BOY
IN THE
TOWER

www.randomhousechildrens.co.uk

Polly Ho-Yen was born in Northampton and brought up in Buckinghamshire.
After working in publishing for several years, she now works as a primary school teacher. Somewhere in between five o'clock in the morning and sitting down in front of a classroom of five-year-olds, *Boy in the Tower* was written. She lives in South London with her husband and their very vocal cat, Milo.

BOY
IN THE
TOWER

POLLY HO-YEN

DOUBLEDAY

BOY IN THE TOWER
A DOUBLEDAY BOOK 978 0 857 53303 6

Published in Great Britain by Doubleday,
an imprint of Random House Children's Publishers UK
A Random House Group Company

This edition published 2014

1 3 5 7 9 10 8 6 4 2

Set in ITC New Baskerville

Random House Children's Publishers UK,
61–63 Uxbridge Road, London W5 5SA

www.**randomhousechildrens**.co.uk
www.**totallyrandombooks**.co.uk
www.**randomhouse**.co.uk

Addresses for companies within The Random House Group Limited
can be found at: www.randomhouse.co.uk/offices.htm

THE RANDOM HOUSE GROUP Limited Reg. No. 954009

A CIP catalogue record for this book is available from the British Library.

Printed and bound in Great Britain by Clays Ltd, St Ives plc

For the first people who read *Boy in the Tower*:
To my dad and Dan.

PART ONE

Before

Chapter One

When you wish that a Saturday was actually a Monday, you know there is something seriously wrong.

I look at the ceiling. At the spot of flaky paint and the stain that looks like a wobbly circle, and at the swaying, wispy spider's web, and I think of all those cold, grey Mondays when I had to make myself get up for school. I would have to force my legs off the mattress and I'd dress in a daze, unwilling to believe it was time to be upright again.

I wish I could wake up to another Monday like that.

Those days are gone now that the Bluchers are here.

When they first arrived, they came quietly and stealthily, as if they tiptoed silently into the world when we were all looking the other way.

I guess I was one of the first people to see them. It's not something I'm proud of. When you know the kind of terrible destruction that just one clump of Bluchers can cause, you wouldn't want to have been there first either.

I think the reason I knew about them before most other people was because I used to spend a lot of my time sitting on my windowsill, looking down over the world. I could see everything from there: the miniature-looking roads, the roofs of the buildings, the broccoli-tops of the trees. And then, of course, the Bluchers themselves and the devastation that followed in their path.

The view has changed so much now that sometimes I wonder if I just made up everything that came before. I have to make myself remember what I used to see: the shops and the bustle, the cars and the people, the red-brick walls of my school and the grey patch of the playground.

Some people say you shouldn't live in the past. But I can't stop putting things into two boxes in my head: Before and After. And it's much easier to think about the Before things.

Before, if there was a day when I didn't go into school because I was ill or Mum wasn't well, I used to sit on my windowsill and watch the other children coming out to play. Everyone would rush out of the tiny black door so fast that I wouldn't be able to tell one little coloured ant from another.

I could always recognize Gaia in the crowd, though. She wore this bright pink coat that stood out a mile. I would see her walking along the edge of the playground. Never in the middle, never in a group. Always walking round and round by herself. Walking in circles.

But like I said, this was all before.

I don't see any other children any more.

I don't know where Gaia is.

Chapter Two

It all began with the rain.

'Don't forget your wellies today, Ade,' Michael's mum would say to me each morning. 'And your proper coat.'

Michael and his family lived in the flat next to ours and we would often hear their voices through the walls. I came to be very familiar with the particular wail that Michael's sister made when she didn't get her own way.

Michael's mum had started knocking for me before school. I now walked there with Michael and his little sister, with their mum shepherding us into the lift and across the road.

I liked them but I preferred walking on my own, to be honest. If I was by myself I could walk along the tops of the walls, trying not to fall off once, which I'd never managed, but Michael's mum didn't like me doing that. She tutted very loudly the first time I tried to step up so I didn't do it again.

It would have been really hard to walk all the way along the wall that week because it had not stopped raining. Everywhere was slick with water. The puddles had grown so big that you had to jump and leap across them and still they grew larger each day. Some of them formed little lakes that were so deep you had to walk all the way around the edge of them. They looked like they might swallow you up if you stepped into them. You couldn't see to their bottom.

I liked the deep, brown-coloured puddles. I liked how you could walk right into them so that your feet would completely disappear.

The first day the rain started falling, we spent most of our playtime doing just that: wading into the murky puddles that had filled any dip or crevice the water could find in the playground.

I remember it was really thundering down all morning, but it had turned into more of a drizzle by lunch time. When we were eating lunch that day, Gaia noticed the teachers all looking out of the windows and having hurried, harassed conversations with each other.

'They're talking about wet play,' she said,

and I looked up from the soggy pile of broccoli I had been wondering if I could get away with not eating. I had piled it up on one side of my plate so that it looked as small as possible.

'Mr Benton is saying that we need to . . . to have a run around,' she continued, and I looked over to the group of teachers who were looking agitatedly around them with their hands on their hips.

'And Miss Farraway is saying only some children have . . . got . . . have got coats. Today. That not everyone's got coats with them today.' Gaia scrunched up her eyes a bit so she could see what they were saying.

She wasn't *listening* to them as such, you see. Gaia was able to understand what most people were saying by looking at how their lips moved. I think it all started because she couldn't hear very well when she was younger and now, even though she has something inside her ear to help her hear, she still does it all the time. The person has to be looking her way, of course, so she can see their lips moving. Sometimes it's not always completely right but she can usually get the gist of what they are saying.

'OK. We are going outside. Mr Benton's

getting really cross and saying that it's more important that we have fresh air . . . than . . . if we are . . . if we are wearing . . . coats. Yep. It's outside play.'

Just a few minutes after that, they blew the whistle and told everyone it was outside play today and to wear a coat if you had one.

Gaia smiled at me. Just a small one. She wasn't showing off or anything but we both liked how her lip-reading meant that we often knew what was going on before everyone else. We'd found out about all sorts of things that way. We discovered that Mr Weaver and Miss Brown were living together after Gaia saw them bickering over what takeaway to order for tea. (Miss Brown wanted Chinese and Mr Weaver, fish and chips.) We even found out what Mr Benton's first name was when Mr Chelmsford, the head teacher, was chatting to him in the corridor. It was something we would never have guessed in a hundred years: Gordon.

The playground was grey and cold but full of shrieks and cries of everyone playing in the puddles. I looked around for Gaia. She had come out before me while I was made to force the last of the broccoli into my mouth. In the end, it hadn't tasted of anything much at all. Just wetness. Green wetness.

Gaia was by one of the larger puddles and I ran over to join her. She was standing at the very edge of it so I thought that if she wasn't careful, she would fall right in. She wasn't wearing wellies or anything and I saw her dip the black rounded toe of her shoe into the water and then quickly bring it back out again. Then she did the same with the other foot.

Just as she did that, at the very moment she dipped her other foot in, a group of kids barged right past her. She had to take a few steps forward, just to keep her balance. Right into the middle of the puddle.

I'd caught up to her by this point.

'Did you get wet, Gaia?' I asked. We both looked down at her shiny, soaked black shoes. Then we looked at each other.

Her face broke into a smile first and before we knew it, we were both laughing so hard that it didn't matter about anyone else in the whole world. You know how sometimes when you laugh, you feel like that? We were laughing and laughing and people splashed us with puddle water and pushed into us, but we didn't care.

'Miss Farraway's saying this . . . is . . . this is madness. Why they . . . let them . . . come outside, I don't know. They're all . . . soaked.' Gaia and I had taken shelter underneath the old shed. Everyone was wet now. I don't mean just a little bit wet, I mean sodden, wet right through. Gaia was watching the adults on duty carefully so we could find out if they were going to send us back inside.

'Mrs Brook's saying it's almost now. No . . . it's almost over now. Let's get . . . everyone . . . under the shed until the . . . Oh, she's looked away.'

Quickly, we moved to the benches at the back just before Mrs Brook blew the whistle and everyone stampeded under the shed. It was the best place to stand, you see. You got a little bit more space.

After that day, we weren't allowed to go outside to play. Instead, we had to spend each playtime watching films on a screen in the hall. We would all bundle onto the floor in an uneasy, fidgeting mass. The windows would steam up so we couldn't see the rain coming down, but we could still hear it. The teachers would turn up the volume high so the film was blaring, but it couldn't block out the pitter-patter of the rain on the roof.

I remember the thunder too. It would come in the afternoons mostly. The dark grey clouds would roll in from the distance and everyone would shriek when they heard the deep rumbles. We didn't get a lot of work done on those afternoons.

I can't clearly remember how many days it went on for, but people were saying things like it was the wettest month on record and were comparing it to a monsoon in India and things like that. All I can say is that it didn't ever stop. Even when you thought it wasn't raining any more, if you looked carefully out of the window you could still see the drops in the puddles. They made little circles in the water. It got to the point where you never felt properly dry, even if you were tucked up in bed at night.

The sound of water was all around us. Buildings sprang leaks, so not only did you hear the fall of the rain outside but also the loud, steady drips landing in buckets and bowls and pans.

Gaia liked the rain. She said it made her feel awake. Sometimes she would point her face up towards the sky and let the raindrops land on her and trickle down her cheeks, like tears. Some of the other children couldn't understand what she was doing and would laugh at her. But I knew it was because she liked the feeling. Just like how I loved balancing on the tops of walls.

I think it was because of this – because we sort of understood things like that – that we were only really friends with each other.

I liked other kids well enough, but sometimes there seemed to be some sort of invisible barrier between us which I didn't know how to make go away. Like with Michael. We walked to school every day for weeks, swinging our bags together as we walked side by side, but we never really spoke. I don't know now if I ever tried to start a conversation, but all I can really remember is the sound of our footsteps in a steady beat, in place of the sound of our voices.

I don't know when I first properly met Gaia, but I can't remember a time when she was not there.

I think our mums were friends first, and although they'd stopped seeing each other, I still saw Gaia every day at school. She didn't live in my block, though. Her tower sat across the road from mine but we both lived on the seventeenth floor. We liked that.

Our blocks looked almost identical, but not quite. When I was younger I thought that a giant, just like the one in *Jack and the Beanstalk*, could have come along and plucked both of our blocks from the ground and joined them together as neatly as two pieces of Lego. They just looked like they would fit together.

But I don't believe in man-eating giants any more. Or beanstalks that grow up and up into the clouds and lead to strange, dangerous lands. I know now that there are things far more terrible. That are far more real.

Chapter Three

One of the things I like best about our flat is that you can see just about anything from the window. You just need to know where to look.

I could always see the old man who slept on a bench in the park with no shoes on, and the delivery van that parked on the pavement to bring crates of milk to the little row of shops. I could even see the little grey bodies of the two thin dogs who walked behind their owner, in a line, every morning. I came to recognize diff-erent people and even knew what sort of time I would see them.

I always liked spotting new things, though. And things that you wouldn't be able to see if you walked past on the street but that only I could see, from high up. Did you know, for instance, that buses have numbers and letters on the top of them? They are painted so large that I could read them from my window.

I didn't only look down, though. I liked to see what was happening in the sky too. I thought that the tiny little aeroplanes that moved across the sky resembled pencils sailing through the air. It didn't seem real to me that they were full of people. They looked so narrow and small up there.

'That's because they're far away, Ade,' a teacher told me once, when I said this.

I didn't reply that it wasn't that I didn't understand. It just amazed me that people could be so high up in the air, in just a little metal capsule with wings.

In those days, I thought that being high up in my tower was safe. There were the flats below mine and the flats below those ones and the ones below them, all holding me up. There was no chance that I could have dropped to the ground. But there was nothing to hold an aeroplane up.

Mum loved the view from our flat too.

'Just think, Ade. Some people would pay to see this but it's ours. All ours. Whenever we want it. All we need to do is look out of the window.'

We would sit together, side by side, watching the world go by, finding pictures in the clouds in the sky. We used to do that all the time.

It's been weeks and weeks since that happened but I can still remember the last time exactly. I had come into the sitting room, swinging my school bag and humming a song that Gaia had heard on the radio and would sing under her breath all the time, without realizing it. I don't really like to sing out loud in front of anyone else, even my mum and Gaia. I usually just do it in my head, but I didn't think Mum would be there.

'That's beautiful, Ade. Come and sing to me.'

I looked up to see Mum sitting by the window. Her eyes looked a bit red and she was wearing a dress that I hadn't seen in a long time but for some reason made me think of bedtimes in the summer. The times when you go to bed and it is still light outside and you have the funny tiredness in your head that comes from playing in the sun all day.

'Sit with me. Tell me about your day.'

I dumped my bag on the floor and went to sit next to her. She rested her hand on my head, as if she was checking to see if I was ill.

'What did you do at school today?'

'Nothing.'

'Nothing? Again? I see,' she said.

'What did you do today, Mum?'

She looked at me mischievously, her eyes twinkling.

'Today?' she said. 'Nothing.'

She laughed and gave me a little knock-knock on the head and went into the kitchen. She came back out holding a couple of bowlfuls of chocolate ice cream. 'Here you go, pet. Sometimes doing nothing can be tiring,' she said, handing me a spoon and a bowl.

It was funny, because when my mum gave me the ice cream, all I could think was: *Where did she get it from?*

Chapter Four

I should tell you a little bit about my mum. She's not like other mums in some ways. And in others, she definitely is.

She tells me to brush my teeth. Sometimes she reads to me just before I fall asleep. She has a beautiful face that tells people who haven't met her before that she is kind but also that she is funny. I think she has the loveliest smile I have ever seen. It's the kind that creeps up on you, and then before you know it her whole face is lit up by it and it beams down on you as well.

Mum's the one who came up with my name. I mean, I know that everyone's mum gives them their name, but when I was in Reception, there were two of us called Adeola and a fair few named Adesoye and Adeyemi and Adefemi, so my mum just said to call me Ade.

Add-ee.

'Nice and simple,' Mum said.

Everyone calls me that now. I think they've forgotten my full name.

Adeola feels a little bit alien even to me now. Only sometimes, Gaia says something like, 'Adeola, I wasn't finished talking, you know,' if she gets cross with me for interrupting and it takes me a second to realize that she's actually talking to me.

The thing with my mum is, she doesn't like going out of the flat much. She doesn't go out at all, actually. It's something that has made us change the way we do things so I've learned pretty much to get along with it.

I remember a time when she sat me down and had a big talk with me about being grown up now, which meant that I could walk to school by myself. Not long after that, she said I'd been so grown up that I could do the shopping that week and we wrote out a list together. Then came the day when she gave me her bank card.

'You are going to have to look all around you, Ade, and wait until there's no one about. If someone suddenly comes up to you, then you'll have to walk away and go back later. You understand?'

'Yes,' I said. Part of me knew that this was a little bit dangerous, that it wasn't something I was meant to do, but mostly I just felt that Mum was trusting me. It was a good feeling.

'So, tell me what you do. If there's no one around.'

'I put the card in the machine. And then I put the pin code in: 5-4-3-7. Then I press the button for cash and then I press the button for £50 and then I wait.'

'And then you take the money. Don't forget that part, Ade! The money will come through the little slot at the bottom. Then you come straight back to me.'

'I won't forget the money, Mum. You must think I'm really stupid!' I was just trying to make a joke but Mum looked at me strangely.

'Don't ever say that. I don't think you're stupid. Not one little bit. Don't let me catch you saying anything like that again, OK? You must never think you're stupid.'

I swallowed hard and looked away. Mum didn't usually talk to me like that. It was like she was talking right up close into my face.

Getting the money from the cash machine was easy enough, though. I did exactly as Mum told me and I never had any problems. I wouldn't say I enjoyed it. I always felt quite worried walking home in case something silly happened, like the wind blew the money out of my hand or something. The notes always felt silky and smooth in my hand at first, but by the time I'd made it back to the tower, they were crumpled and warm from being clenched in my sweaty palm. But I felt something like pride, something like happiness, when I delivered the money to Mum.

'Good boy, Ade,' Mum said the first time I got back from the cash point, and she smiled at me. It was a small, quick one, her lips drawing upwards hurriedly, but it made my heart swell up. I hadn't seen Mum smile in a long time.

'Right, now, take this.' She shoved one of the crumpled bank notes back into my hand. 'And here's a list. Hurry back.'

I looked down at Mum's scrawled handwriting on the back of an old envelope. *Large milk, white bread, spag hoops, Frosties.*

She was looking at me so expectantly and I knew she wasn't asking me, she was telling me. *Take this. Hurry back.* So I went, and when I dumped the blue-and-white striped bag full of shopping on the floor, Mum rewarded me with an even longer smile and I knew that I would do anything to make her smile again.

It seemed to start slowly with the not-walking-me-to-school and the not-going-shopping and the not-getting-money, and then, before I knew it, I realized I hadn't seen Mum leave the flat for a couple of months. After that, Mum asked me to make dinner one night, and the night after that and the night after that. It was only heating a tin of something up in a pan and toasting a few pieces of bread. I didn't mind doing it.

But I decided to tell Gaia about it. I wanted to find out if her mum was asking her to do the same sort of things.

I can remember exactly the day I told Gaia.

It was the day the rain stopped falling.

The day the first building fell.

Chapter Five

'It's too hot to eat this,' said Gaia. We were sitting in the hall with plates of roast dinner in front of us. A thin slice of meat, two greasy-looking potatoes and bright orange circles of carrot that were all floating in a pool of brown gravy.

The day the rain stopped was one of the hottest that we'd had in ages. It was funny after all the soggy raincoats and wet socks, to find yourself feeling too hot all of a sudden. Everyone had basked in the sunshine during playtime and lain down on the black tarmac to rest.

Gaia was right. It felt too hot even to eat. The sun was shining in through the hall windows so I had to squint when I looked up at her.

'I'm going to make a run for it,' Gaia said, standing up.

'Gaia,' I said. 'Can I ask you something?'

She sat back down again.

'Does your mum ask you to do the shopping sometimes?' I said.

'What do you mean?'

'My mum's asked me to do that now. Do you do it?'

Gaia's eyes narrowed ever so slightly.

'What do you mean, she's asked you to do it?'

I realized that now I'd brought it up, Gaia wouldn't leave me alone until she knew every little detail, so I told her what had been going on. From the very first time Mum had sat me down to tell me to walk to school by myself to the time she gave me her bank card.

I didn't tell Gaia everything, though.

But I still wasn't prepared for the worried, frowning look that took over her face.

'You shouldn't be doing that.'

'Mum says I'm grown up now. She says I do a really good job.'

'But . . . but . . . if you're doing all of those things, then what's your mum doing?'

It was a good question. Mostly, she was sleeping. At the same time she stopped leaving the flat, she started feeling really tired all the time.

'I just need to sleep, baby,' Mum would say, and I would close the bedroom door behind me and not come in and sit down on the bed and tell her all about the nothing I had been doing at school that day.

'When did you start doing this?' Gaia asked.

I speared a piece of meat on my fork. It dripped gravy onto the plate, each drop making a little circular splash just like raindrops falling into puddles.

'Ade?' Gaia said softly.

It had been many months since the day I came home to hear Mum crying. Crying is probably the wrong word, although she certainly *was* crying. Tears were running all the way down her face and they fell from the tip of her chin onto a growing patch of wetness on her skirt. But it was also like moaning. And shouting. And screaming. And wailing. All mixed up together.

It was a sound that terrified me.

'Mum,' I said. But my voice was lost in the sound of Mum's cries. In the end, I put my hand onto her shoulder, and only then did she turn to look at me.

She looked right through me as if I wasn't there and then her eyes seemed to focus on me and take in who I was. She reached out for me and clasped me tightly, too tightly, to her.

'It's all right,' she said, over and over again. 'It's all right, it's all right.' But she didn't stop crying.

I felt like I was the one who should have been saying that to her, because as she looked at me then, I could see her face clearly.

She was hurt. One of her eyes was so swollen that it wasn't able to open properly and the other was bruised and half open. There was a violent purple bump on her forehead. A weeping gash cut across her cheek. It looked like a wicked gaping smile.

'What happened? What happened?' I said but Mum didn't answer me. Her face creased as she sobbed harder, and the cut on her face looked like it was crying too.

'Mummy?' I said, although I didn't know what I was asking until the words were on my lips: 'Who did this?'

'Oh, Ade,' Mum was whispering under her breath. 'Oh, Ade, oh, Ade.'

I started crying then too, even though I wished myself not to. I wished I had rang up the police and an ambulance. I wished I'd got something to make Mum's face feel better. I wished I was able to do something other than howl into Mum's shoulder as she rocked us both back and forth, trying to make us forget she was so badly injured. But for all my wishing, I let myself huddle down into her lap and cry desperate tears for what had happened.

We fell asleep like that, locked together, but when I woke up, Mum was gone from the bedroom and the room was dark.

'Mum?' My voice sounded very small and alone in the dim light.

'I'm . . .' Mum's voice sounded hoarse and sore. 'I'm in here.'

She was sitting on the sofa in the darkness. I felt glad that there were no lights on so I wouldn't have to look at her poor mangled face, and then I felt ashamed of myself.

'Mum!' I cried out like she had been lost to me, and I climbed into her lap once more and buried my face into the soft fabric of her jacket. It struck me then that she hadn't even taken her coat off all this time.

'It's all right, Ade. It's all right. Go back to sleep,' Mum said. And I did.

I knew that something bad had happened but I couldn't ask Mum what it was. I tried to. I really did. But I couldn't force the words out of my mouth.

I felt scared. Scared wondering why Mum had been so terribly hurt. Scared that it would happen again. Perhaps that was one of the reasons I didn't mind doing the shopping: at least if I did it, I knew nothing bad would happen to Mum. She was safe if she was at home.

I didn't tell anybody about what had happened, not even Gaia. I didn't want it to be real, and if I didn't tell anyone then that stopped it becoming more real, didn't it? I think Mum felt the same, and that's why she didn't tell the police or go to hospital.

Mum did start to get better, in some ways. Her face started healing straight away. It went very purple and then a sort of blue and after that it was very yellowy. You could still see the scar on her cheek but it stopped looking painful. I thought things would go back to how they were before, back when Mum used to tell me funny things that had happened at the shop she worked in. She was always so good at describing customers, it felt like they appeared right in front of me. Or when she would open the fridge and then slam it back shut again and say, 'Ade, let's get out of here,' and we'd go to McDonald's for a treat.

But instead Mum retreated into herself, locking herself away from the outside world.

Gaia somehow seemed to understand all this, without me even having to say it. 'Maybe your mum's got something wrong with her,' she said gently, cutting through my memories.

I screwed up my face when she said this, so I knew she tried to stop herself from saying the next words on her mind, but they came tumbling out anyway: 'Maybe she should see a doctor?'

It was only in a whisper, but I heard it.

A doctor. Someone to make Mum better again. It seemed like a good idea. Her face had mended itself but there was damage on the inside, wounds I couldn't see, that needed healing as well.

When I came home from school that day I went straight into her bedroom and said in a loud voice, 'Mum, I'm home.' She stirred in her sleep and then gave a sort of shrug that buried her body deeper into the bedclothes.

'Wake up, Mum,' I said. 'I'm home. I'm home.'

There was a stale smell in Mum's bedroom. It wasn't unpleasant exactly, but neither was it clean or fresh. An image of Mum, ready for work, appeared in my mind. Her clothes were neat and they smelled nice, like flowers, and what I think clouds might smell like.

'Ade,' she said in a small voice. 'Be a good boy and go and play in the sitting room, will you? I'm so, so tired. I've got to sleep some more. Then I'll come out, OK?'

'You're always tired all the time,' I said. 'Mum, do you think you should go and see someone?'

'Someone? What do you mean?' Mum's voice sounded sharp, like the screech of a violin.

'Someone . . . like a doctor,' I said.

'I'm just tired, Ade. I have to sleep,' she said. 'That will make me feel better. A doctor can't help me.' Just saying those few words seemed to make her more tired.

'They might, Mum.'

In answer, Mum rolled away from me. I walked round to the side of the bed she was facing. She wasn't even asleep. She was just staring at the wall. Maybe all this time I'd thought she was sleeping when she wasn't. She was just staring at the walls, unmoving.

'Mum,' I said, but her face remained expressionless. 'Mum!' I insisted, but she didn't even flinch. 'Get up. You have to! You have to go to work!' Again I thought of Mum dressed up all nicely, like she used to be.

At first I thought she hadn't heard me but then I saw round, swollen tears roll down her cheeks.

'I can't, Ade. I can't go out there.'

'But what about your job?'

'I told them I'm not going back. It happened . . . it happened . . .' Mum's breathing was quickening as though she couldn't get enough air. 'It happened just by the shop.'

'What did, Mum?' I said. 'What happened?' I'd not dared to ask her that again since the night I'd come home to find her bleeding and injured.

'They were there,' she said simply, and she rolled over, away from me, and her shoulders shook with her sobs. I put my hand on her and felt the vibrations up my arm, all her pain racking her body. After a long time she was still and I trod softly out of the room and left her to sleep.

Before she started crying, I'd felt cross with her and I hated it. Part of me knew she couldn't help it but another voice had whispered into my ear: *Is she trying to get better? Why won't she try to get up?*

But now, I only felt achingly sad and alone.

I switched the television on and turned the volume up high so Mum would hear it through the walls. We used to watch television together all the time. She'd watch my programmes and I'd watch some of hers too. She used to really like cookery shows so I flicked through the channels to see if I could find one. If she couldn't see it, she could at least hear what they were cooking.

There was nothing like that on, though, so I put on the news. They were talking about an old abandoned pub that had fallen down. I recognized the pub straight away. It was right by my tower. I walked right past it to go to one of the bigger shops. It was one of those tall, old-fashioned pubs but it had been empty for a while and its windows had been boarded up. Last time I'd walked past I'd noticed that plants had started growing out from in between the bricks. They had grey-green leaves and purple flowers that clumped together to look a bit like an ice-cream cone.

It was reported as just one of those strange, bizarre happenings that no one could explain.

Someone or other was cross because they had just bought it and had big plans for it. And now it was just a pile of rubble.

Then the newsreaders started talking about something different and I realized how loud the voices from the television were and I felt bad that I had turned up the volume so high in the first place. I pressed the *down* button on the remote control and made the voices get quieter and quieter until they disappeared altogether.

Then I sat in silence, just watching the pictures, trying to work out what people were saying by how their lips moved, like Gaia could.

But I couldn't understand them.

Chapter Six

I didn't give up trying to talk Mum into getting help.

The next day she was up and tried to give me a shopping list but I wouldn't take it unless she came with me.

'Come on, Ade,' she said when I refused to put out my hand for the fluttering piece of paper. 'The bread's gone green. You don't want to eat green bread, do you? I know I don't.'

'Why don't we go together and we could go to the doctor's afterwards?' I asked.

Mum didn't say anything. She just started taking little gasps of air and tried not to look at me. But she did catch my eye as she took those little, painful breaths, and in that tiny moment I could tell that she was blaming me for making her breathe like that because I'd asked her to go with me. I snatched the list from her hand and ran out of the flat and went down in the lift and across the road to get the food. It was only when I'd gotten all the way to the shop that I realized I'd forgotten to bring any money with me.

'I'm sorry, Ade,' Mum said as soon as I came back in. She was still standing in exactly the same position as when I'd left, as if she'd been frozen the whole time I was away. 'I know this can't be fun for you.'

I didn't say anything but just reached up to the jam jar where we kept our money and took out a five-pound note that had been folded tightly in half again and again until it was only a little square.

I couldn't look Mum in the eye. I felt like I'd failed her and it was an unbearable feeling, a pressure that had settled over my chest and wouldn't let up.

'Let's go together. It's a good idea,' she said.

I looked up at her sharply. She looked like she might start crying but she was also nodding a little, as if to say, *Yes, yes, I can do this.*

'Are you sure, Mum?' I couldn't believe it. I felt too glad even to smile.

Mum gave me another of her funny nods. She stood up a little unsteadily and, holding my hand, she walked towards the front door.

Every step was an effort and I was reminded of the way a snail moves, those tiny movements propelling it forward bit by bit. I felt so happy as she took those few shuffling steps past our front door but also daunted by the task that lay ahead. The shops and the doctor's surgery seemed very far away. It was as if we had just begun to climb a mountain and we couldn't see the top because it was surrounded by thick, white clouds.

We'd made it as far as the lifts when she started doing the funny breathing again. Her hand tightened around mine and I tried to give her a reassuring squeeze back but I don't think she felt it, she was holding on so tightly.

'I can't do it, Ade. I'm sorry, I can't.'

As she turned back to our flat, her eyes met mine for the briefest moment, and again they seemed to say, *Don't make me do this, this is hurting me.*

And just like that I was standing on my own in the corridor with the sound of our front door slamming, echoing in the emptiness.

I did the shopping and I almost made it home without crying, apart from when the woman in the shop put a lollipop in my bag along with the bread and milk and said, 'Looks like you need one, love.'

'Thank you,' I said.

'You're welcome, honey,' she said, and I shocked myself when my eyes filled with tears.

I quickly ran out, leaving the whole five-pound note on the counter without waiting for my change just so I wouldn't have to talk to the kind woman any more.

I walked past the old pub that had fallen down. It was a pile of bricks but I could just about make out the sign that was sticking out of the bricks. It had a picture of a man's face on it. I'd forgotten that had even happened, I had been so worried about Mum.

When I finally got home, Mum was back in bed. I didn't go in to check on her. I wanted to believe that she was sleeping, not lying awake in the dark, waiting for the morning to come.

Chapter Seven

I knew what I needed to do to make it easier for
Mum, so I went back to doing all the things I did
before.

Before I tried to make Mum come outside
with me, I'd got really good at being quiet when
I arrived home from school so I didn't wake her.
I called it the Silence Game.

I had all sorts of tactics. One of the things I
did was leave the hat off our whistling kettle
when I boiled water for tea. Another was
tiptoeing around the flat as quietly as I could,
before I realized that I made a lot less noise if I
just walked very carefully and slowly and spread
my weight over the soles of my feet. That way I
could stop any floorboards creaking.

I also made sure that I didn't flush the toilet
after I'd used it. I know that sounds a little bit
disgusting but I just put the lid down straight

away and it wasn't too bad. Then Mum flushed it when she got up.

Sometimes I would get a surprise and find something lying around that meant Mum must have left the flat that day. It didn't happen often but enough to make me excited every day that I might find a clue that she had managed to go outside. Once it was just that her shoes were a little bit wet on their soles. I used to check the bottoms of her shoes every day, you see. Sometimes it was something that was left out, that had not been there before. You would not believe how happy I felt when a single orange appeared on our sofa one day. Or how fantastically pleased I was when I found a newspaper sitting on the kitchen table. The time gaps in between finding things like that were getting longer and longer but it still gave me a lot of hope.

Then there were the precious few days when Mum really would surprise me. She would be awake when I came home from school. Sometimes she had even washed her face and put lipstick on. Then she would blow me away by casually producing something that hadn't come from any of my shopping trips, and that she couldn't even have bought from one of the shops close to the flat.

The day she presented me with a bowl of chocolate ice cream set my mind racing. I knew she must have gone to the supermarket, because it was the only place you could get this particular flavour, which had bits of chocolate brownie and swirls of caramel in it. It was our favourite. Before Mum got hurt, we used to eat it all the time. 'Too much of the time!' Mum would laugh, in the old days, before patting the rounds of our bellies.

She could have quite easily just bought some chocolate or sweets from the nearby newsagent's, but she hadn't. She'd walked right past it and gone all the way down the road to buy our favourite chocolate ice cream. Chocolate ice cream for me. The ice cream said, *I'm getting better, Ade, I really am* – and you know what? It tasted all the better because of it.

There were no signs that she had left the flat the day after she'd tried to come shopping with me. Everything was lying untouched and silent when I got home that night.

I started playing the Silence Game and slowly walked over to the window ledge. I didn't make a sound.

I looked down on the city below me and found the spot where the old pub had fallen down.

I might only be saying this because I know what's happened since, but I thought I did notice some things that were a little bit odd about that mound of rubble.

Looking at it from my window, I thought I could see a faint blue tinge in the space where it had once stood. And it was strange that there was so little of it left, too. Not really what you'd expect from a big, tall building.

I remember thinking that someone must have already started clearing it away. And that the blue tinge was just a trick of the light. I didn't know at the time that these were all important details.

I did put the pub into my scrapbook, though. I drew a picture of what it used to look like and what it looked like now it had fallen down. I wrote down the name as well. It was called The George.

During the last school holidays, Miss Farraway had given each of us a large green scrapbook to draw or write about things that we saw around us.

'Anything?' I'd asked her.

'Anything you see that is interesting, Ade,' she'd said. 'Or you can stick things in. If you find something you like the look of.'

She called them our Eye Spy books. I hadn't filled mine up with much so far. I'd only stuck in a bit of a Happy Meal box that I'd had once and drawn the buildings I could see from my window. It was hard to draw the straight lines of the towers, though. They always came out wobbly.

Now I'd drawn the pub too.

How was I to know that this was only the beginning?

Chapter Eight

There was one person other than me and Gaia who knew about my mum, and that was Michael's mum.

There was a time, a couple of weeks before I told Gaia, when I stopped going into school for a few days because Mum stopped getting out of bed and I didn't want to leave her.

I knew something was wrong because she had stopped eating.

She forgot to flush the toilet when she got up to go, too. The smell was getting really bad, so in the end I had to flush it anyway.

It had been days and days since I had found anything that showed me that she'd left the flat. I always spent the first twenty minutes after coming home searching and searching for any sign that she'd made it outside. I was getting desperate to find a clue that she was getting better.

I knew she wasn't eating because I'd always bring her a bowl of cereal in the morning and some more food in the evening and the plates were all left untouched.

It was a little bit like years ago on Christmas Eve when I'd put some biscuits out for Santa and they were still sitting there in the morning, just as I had left them. I asked Gaia what happened at her house and she said that all she was left with was a few crumbs and the stump of a carrot.

The same sort of thing happened with the tooth fairy. I kept putting my teeth under my pillow but they were always still there in the morning. Gaia said that maybe there was a problem with my block because she got a silver fifty-pence coin for every tooth.

Now I know differently.

On one of the days I was off school, we'd run out of food and money, so I left the flat with Mum's cash card. I knew I shouldn't have. I had a twinge of worry about what would happen if someone I knew saw me, but I put that fear to the back of my mind because I was hungry and hadn't eaten since the day before.

I waited behind a tree until an old man with a walking stick had finished at the cash point.

He took a long time, but once he'd hobbled off I couldn't see anyone else on the street and I tapped in Mum's pin code and waited for the money to appear in the little letter box.

'Ade!' Someone said my name just as the machine started bleeping at me to take the money.

I didn't turn round to see who it was. I just grabbed the money and ran back home as fast as I could. I didn't go to the shops, and all afternoon I tried to ignore the rumblings in my stomach.

A few hours later, there was a knock on the door. I wasn't going to answer it, but then I heard Michael's mum say, 'I know you're in there, Ade. Open up.' When I still didn't open the door, she added, 'I saw you at the cash point today, y'know. I need to speak to your mother.' I opened the door then.

She spent a long time in Mum's bedroom and I tried to listen through the door to what they were talking about but they spoke in such low voices, I couldn't pick out any words.

Then she took me next door to her house for dinner.

We ate chicken and rice and I had to sit next to Michael's little sister, who kept poking me in the side with her pink plastic fork. Michael wouldn't look me in the eye. I don't think he wanted me to be there and he was just trying to pretend that it wasn't really happening.

There was a sweet, sticky sauce all over the chicken. It was delicious. A lot better than any-thing I was able to make myself. I ate greedily, licking my fingers clean when I had finished until I noticed Michael's mum looking at me with a worried frown on her face.

The next day, Michael's mum turned up at my front door at quarter to nine. There had been no explanation and Mum hadn't said any-thing to me about it but I knew I had no choice but to go with her.

'Ade, you ready?' she would call out to me. 'We're going.' I would have to run to catch up with the three figures of Michael's mum, Michael and his sister disappearing round the corner. They never waited for me, they just expected me to catch up with them before they got to the lifts.

'Ade, you ready? We're going.'

The same, every day. Always at the same time, each day. Every day until they closed the school down, right around the time the rain stopped and everything changed.

Chapter Nine

I sort of liked school. I liked that you always knew what was coming next. You just had to look at the timetable for the day on the board to find out. I also liked that our teacher, Miss Farraway, was always there, no questions asked. She would come and collect us from the playground at nine o'clock every single day, with the same sort of smile on her face each time, and there was not a day when she wouldn't turn up.

The thing I liked most about school was Gaia.

I liked nothing more than to see her smile or to make her laugh and I never got more upset than when she got hurt by someone.

Like on the day we planted our seeds.

I'll never forget it.

Everyone at school had been talking about a warehouse that had fallen down, just like the pub. Some children had walked right past it to come to school and they were telling us about the broken glass and the funny bits of metal that were left in place of where the warehouse had once stood.

We were talking so much that Miss Farraway had to clap her hands together to stop our chatter. When we were quiet she announced that we would plant sunflower seeds today. I didn't have to look at Gaia's face to know that she was smiling.

Gaia loved growing things. She told me once about a little garden she had made on her windowsill. She had a little pot of mint and an old house plant her mum was going to throw away when it looked like it was dead, but that Gaia had brought back to life. She would collect bits for it all the time, too. A green leaf from the pavement or a prickly conker case and its shiny brown conker. I'd never seen her little garden but I could picture it perfectly in my head.

We were working on different tables that day. I had picked out my orange flower pot and I was trying to scratch my name onto it. It wasn't working, though. The pencil wouldn't make a mark on the plastic, however hard I pressed down.

Then I looked at the others on my table and I saw that they were all writing their names on white labels. I put my pencil down and tried to cover the dents and lines I had made on my pot with my sleeve. I looked everywhere for the labels but I couldn't see them anywhere. By now everyone else was chatting about something else. I couldn't ask them. I was going to have to put my hand up and ask Miss Farraway and then explain why I had not listened in the first place.

I never meant *not* to listen, but sometimes when someone apart from my mum or Gaia was talking to me, I felt like I was floating away, far up above where they were. Their voice would become very muffled, so I couldn't make out the words they were saying. A lot of teachers used to get quite cross with me when this happened. They would bellow, 'You are not listening!' at me to make me pay attention. Miss Farraway was not like that. She was much kinder and sometimes would repeat things several times, just for me. It still didn't stop it from happening, though.

I was just about to put my hand up when Gaia caught my eye and raised her eyebrows at me as if to ask, *Are you OK?*

I mouthed, 'Labels,' as clearly as I could, so

she would be able to read my lips. She gave me a little nod and stood up from her table and went up to Miss Farraway's desk where there was a pile of white labels in a little green basket.

'Gaia, haven't you already had one of those?' Miss Farraway asked.

'I made a mistake, so I need another one,' Gaia replied, and Miss Farraway nodded and turned away. Gaia dropped the label in front of me as she went back to sit down, and I quickly wrote my name on it and stuck it onto my pot so that it looked just like everyone else's.

'Thank you,' I mouthed to Gaia. 'I owe you.'

She just smiled and looked away.

After that, we filled our pots with soil. It was sticky and black and smelled of the outside when it rains. I liked the feeling of it between my fingers. I could see that Gaia did too because she, like me, was playing with it. She was taking a pinchful of soil between her fingers and then rubbing it together so that it fell into the pot like snow.

'Miss Farraway, Gaia's making a mess!' some-one from her table called out.

'Gardening's a messy business – you have to get your hands dirty,' said Miss Farraway. 'But it's better to be outside to get really messy. Can you stop that in here, Gaia? Thank you.' Gaia nodded, but I could see by the way she sucked in her cheeks ever so slightly that she felt a bit embarrassed.

After that we chose a sunflower seed to plant. One each. I spent a long time choosing mine. It had thick stripes down the middle and then thin ones down the sides. I made a little hole in the soil with my finger for the seed and then covered it up so I could not see it at all.

I looked over at Gaia. She hadn't planted hers yet. She was still holding it in her hand and it looked like she was whispering something under her breath.

'Miss Farraway, Gaia's talking to her seed!' a girl from her table shouted out. The whole class laughed loudly. It took Miss Farraway a few minutes to get everyone to be quiet again. By then, Gaia had shoved her seed into the pot and was looking down at her lap so that I couldn't see her face.

We went out to play not long after that, Gaia marching ahead of me. I hurried after her, but overheard two people talking:

'Did you do it?'

'Yeah, I just went in and Miss wasn't there. She's looking at us right now. Freaky Gaia.' Hearing her name made me stop right behind the two girls.

'Where did you put it?'

'In the bin. She's going to be talking to just an empty pot from now on.'

'Ha!'

'She's such a weirdo.'

'Yeah, she's such a weirdo.'

They were looking right at her as they talked. They couldn't have known she could understand what they were saying from all the way across the playground. Only I could see from the look on her face that she had understood exactly what they had said.

I don't know if I'm a very good friend to Gaia. I felt very, very angry but I'm not the kind of friend who, hearing that, would go up to those girls and say, 'Leave Gaia alone!' and then maybe hit them across the face for being so mean. There are people who are like that but I am not. I'm not even the kind of friend who knows the right thing to say to cheer her up. I didn't run straight over to her and say nice, comforting things that would make her feel better.

I thought about it for a minute before I decided what I would do.

I went back inside and into our classroom. Miss Farraway was still not there but I had to be quick. I went to my pot and pushed the soil away until I found my seed. Then I found Gaia's pot, with her neat, curly writing on it, and I buried the seed deep inside the soil.

In the end, mine was not the only pot that didn't have a little seedling in it. A few others didn't grow at all.

But Gaia's did.

It grew taller than all the rest.

Chapter Ten

The next day, another two buildings had fallen down.

The first was an upholsterer's workshop and the second was actually somebody's house. It was one of those quite small ones which joins onto the houses next to it, in a little row.

We had to walk past it to get to school. It looked a bit like someone had just cut the house out, like how you would take a slice of cake.

I asked Michael's mum who had lived there but she shushed me. She didn't want to talk about it.

'Did you hear about the buildings that have fallen down?' I asked Gaia.

Gaia looked at me as if she was saying, *What do you take me for?*

'Of course I have, Adeola. Everyone's talking about it.'

'Sorry. I know,' I said. 'It's just that Mum hasn't said much about it to me so I wasn't sure . . .' My voice trailed off. What I was going to say was, 'I wasn't sure how big a deal it was.' I know that might sound a bit stupid, but sometimes it's hard until you've spoken to someone else about something to know how serious it is.

Gaia looked at me, softly.

'It's quite bad, Ade. They don't know what's causing it. People are getting scared.'

I looked away from her gaze.

'We just need to wake up tomorrow and hear that nowhere else has fallen down,' she said. 'Then I think everyone will calm down. Did you hear about that little house that fell?'

I shook my head.

'There was an old woman living there. They found her body underneath some bricks.'

We both went quiet for a moment.

'But this is the weird thing,' Gaia continued. 'There weren't nearly enough bricks left where the house fell. There should have been loads and loads more. The same thing happened with the pub and the warehouse and the other place.'

'The workshop,' I said.

'What?'

'The other place was the upholsterer's work-shop.'

'Right, the workshop. So I think someone is taking the bricks.'

'So you think a person is doing this?' I asked. 'To steal bricks?'

'I don't know,' Gaia said. 'But I can't think why else it's happening. Why do you think they are falling?'

'I dunno. I guess I thought there was just something wrong with those buildings.'

'But why those ones? And why is it happening all of a sudden? All at the same time?' Gaia said.

'But why would anyone want to steal bricks like that?'

'I don't know,' Gaia said. 'How about . . . how about . . . because there's a monster . . . who only likes the taste of bricks from Camberwell?'

'Yes!' I said, warming to the idea. 'And he hates the taste of bricks from anywhere else.'

'Yeah, he tried the ones in Elephant and Castle and spat them all out!'

'And don't get him started on the bricks in Peckham, they're far too salty.'

'He only comes out at night because he's very shy about people seeing him eat.'

We laughed at each other.

'He doesn't mean anyone any harm,' I continued. 'He's quite a nice monster, really. He's really sorry about the lady who died.'

Quickly, our grins fell from our faces. It wasn't a joke, a story we had made up. Someone had gone to bed one night thinking everything was OK, but the next morning they wouldn't ever wake up, lying buried under the rubble of their own home.

'I wonder what's really going on,' said Gaia. 'And when is it going to end?'

I didn't say, but there was a question in my mind too: I wondered if more people would get hurt along the way.

It turned out I was right to worry.

Chapter Eleven

That night, our school was on the news. There was the entrance that we went in every day on the screen, just by where the newsreader was standing. It had a stone over the entrance that had BOYS inscribed on it in curly capitals from the olden days when girls and boys had to come in through different doors. The newsreader was saying something about whether our school should be closed down or not.

I raced into Mum's room, flinging the door open so it clanged against the wall.

'Mum! Wake up! My school's on telly!'

There was a funny, stale smell in her room and the curtains were drawn although it was still light outside.

'Mum?' I sat down next to her. She just looked like a lump in the bed. She lay so still that for one moment I wondered whether, if I pulled the covers back, I would find just a pile of cushions and realize Mum had been tricking me this whole time. Maybe she was out at the supermarket this very moment buying the ice cream we liked.

I threw back the pink blanket but there were no pillows, just Mum with her eyes tightly closed, her body compacted together as though she was making herself into a ball. I prodded her but she didn't move, so I shook her, gently at first and then with more force. She moaned and turned onto her front. I was worried she wouldn't be able to breathe if she slept face down, so I turned her back onto her side. She sighed deeply but she didn't wake.

'Mum!' I shouted. 'Mum!'

More loudly this time: 'Mum! Mum! Mum!'

Her eyes flickered and then opened.

'Ade,' she whispered. She tried to moisten her lips.

'Mum! Wake up!'

'What's wrong?'

'My school's on the news. You've got to see it.'

'Not now, Ade. Not now. Get me some water, would you?'

'But we'll miss it,' I said. Remembering what

I had heard, I added, 'And they might close the school down.'

'Oh,' Mum said, and her eyes flickered shut as she fell back to sleep.

When I came back into the sitting room, they'd stopped showing my school but they were still talking about what was happening with the buildings. It ran all night, or at least right up, to where I switched it off to go to bed. They couldn't stop talking about it.

That was when I knew that Gaia was right. People were getting scared. And the only way they would stop feeling scared would be if they woke up the next day and no more buildings had fallen down.

But it didn't happen like that. More and more fell. I saw on the news that some people had died because they'd been sleeping in their beds when the walls had fallen down around them and then their floors had given way.

Lots of people who knew all about how to make houses were on the television talking about foundations, and other people were talking about terror or something like that.

It always seemed to happen at night time, when the buildings would fall. No one had actually *seen* it happen. We just kept waking up in the morning to find out that another and another had gone. It was beginning to look really bad from what I could see from my window. There were all these funny little patches in between the buildings now. More and more each day.

They decided to send in lots of policemen who sat in vans or walked around at night to see if they could find out what was happening. We all watched too. I could see lots of lit-up windows in the blocks around us. In a strange sort of way, I felt less lonely seeing lots of other people looking out of their windows. I wasn't the only one any more. One night I counted seventy-eight faces. We all wanted to find out what was going on.

Chapter Twelve

There was the horrible day when we all had to go for an assembly. All the teachers looked red-eyed and wouldn't meet our stares. Mr Chelmsford told us that Leyla in Year Five and her brother Mehdi in Year One were no longer with us. Their house had collapsed when they were inside it. It took me a moment to realize what he was trying to say.

We couldn't believe that they'd really gone.

It did not seem real at all.

The day after that, the Reception teacher, Mrs Brook, didn't come to school, and instead they had a teacher no one had ever seen before. There was another assembly where they told us that she had died too. Everyone was crying a lot now, not only because we were sad about Leyla, Mehdi and Mrs Brook but because we knew someone else would be next.

In the days that followed, there were always a few more people who we were missing, and eventually we stopped having assemblies.

Chapter Thirteen

Every day, I looked for Gaia.

I could feel the knot in my stomach getting tighter and tighter until I saw her. I didn't realize that she was just as worried about me until one day she said to me, 'Maybe it's not a good idea for you to be walking about after school.'

On the news that morning, they said another five buildings had fallen. It wasn't stopping, as we had all hoped. The number of fallen buildings was getting bigger each day.

'I need to get some more food, though. We're about to run out,' I said.

Although that was what I said, I was actually starting to feel funny about being out on the streets by myself.

For one thing, I would have to walk past a lot of the buildings that had fallen down. In some of them, I knew that the people who had lived inside them had died when the walls and floors collapsed around them.

The real reason, though, was that even though I knew the buildings only seemed to fall down at night, our streets just didn't feel safe any more. Even with the sunshine streaming down. Our little world kept changing and no one knew why.

It felt like Gaia was able to read my mind. She knew exactly what I was thinking.

'I know it always happens at night but things have changed around here,' she said. 'I just think it'd be better if you went with someone else.'

I shook my head. Mum was sleeping as much as ever. She hadn't been outside for a long time. The only other person I could ask was Michael's mum, but I'd accidentally knocked into Michael in the playground a couple of days before and he'd turned round to me, scowling. 'What you do that for?' he'd said.

'Sorry,' I said. 'It was an accident.'

'Just stay away, you hear?'

I'd never really had a conversation with Michael before, if you could call this one, and I was surprised by how quietly he spoke and how angry he sounded.

'OK,' I said.

'I don't know why my mum is looking out for you, but I'm not your friend, all right?'

'OK,' I said again, unsure of what else to say.

'Don't cry, Ade,' Michael said, and he walked off.

I wasn't going to cry but I did feel surprised. Shocked, I suppose. I knew Michael wasn't that keen on me but I didn't realize how much he disliked me.

Gaia said he wasn't worth the brain space but I saw her trip him up on purpose as he walked past in the dining hall.

'Sorry,' she said sweetly, and Michael just scowled in much the same way as he'd scowled at me.

So I wasn't about to start asking his mum for favours.

'Mum's not great at the moment,' I told Gaia.

'I didn't mean your mum,' Gaia said, her eyes shining. 'I'll come with you.'

'No,' I said. I think I shouted it. The last thing I wanted was Gaia close to the fallen buildings. It was funny that we both had the same

strong feeling that we should stay away from
them if we could.

'Anyway,' I went on, 'your mum and dad
wouldn't let you.'

Gaia smiled.

'They don't have to know,' she said.

Chapter Fourteen

'Let's see your list then,' Gaia said as we turned off down the road towards the shops.

The thing is, Mum had stopped giving me lists by then. I knew the right stuff to get, it wasn't a big problem or anything, but I knew Gaia wouldn't approve. When I first started going shopping, Gaia had said that at the very least Mum was making sure I was getting proper food by giving me a list so I wasn't just buying rubbish like crisps and chocolate and nothing else.

I didn't want Gaia to get cross with Mum about it, so I said, 'I get the same things all the time now. I know what to get,' and hoped she'd leave it at that.

She didn't say anything, though, and I felt glad until I realized why she was so quiet.

We were standing in front of one of the fallen buildings.

I'm not sure what it used to be because it had been empty for quite a long time, even before it fell. It was big and had crumbling red bricks and large windows with lots of panes that had been smashed.

Now that it had gone, it was a massive empty space. The police had put up lots of red-and-white tape all around it and we could see a couple of men with yellow hard hats on who were having a look at some of the rubble left on the ground.

'Let's keep going,' I said, and I tugged at Gaia's arm. We kept walking and then we passed the old pub, the first building that had fallen.

Gaia stopped to look but I kept walking, so she had to run to catch up with me.

'Did you notice . . .' Gaia started. I waited but she didn't carry on.

'What?' I asked.

'Did you notice something funny—' Again, she stopped herself. She looked behind her to where the pub once stood. 'I don't know,' she said. 'I don't know.'

'What?' I asked again.

'I thought the bricks looked a bit . . . this is

going to sound really strange. But I thought they looked a bit . . . blue.'

'Blue?'

'I know it sounds weird but I'm sure I saw it.'

'We'll have a look on our way back.'

'OK. Well. It's just . . . I don't know. I get the feeling that we shouldn't hang around there. There's a funny feeling about it.'

I'd felt it too. Was it just because we knew what had happened in those buildings or was it something else? I couldn't explain but I didn't want to stand there for long either. Something was telling me to move away.

We did the shopping as quickly as we could and headed home.

We didn't see anyone on the way back. There was no sign of the two men in the yellow hard hats who'd been sifting through the rubble and we only stopped briefly to look again.

'Maybe,' I said. 'Maybe it *is* a bit blue.'

'Do you think there's something on the bricks?' Gaia said.

'We'd need to get closer to really see.'

'Maybe we could do it tomorrow. After school. Not now.'

'No, not now,' I agreed.

We hurried off down the road.

'Thanks for coming with me,' I said.

'It's OK,' Gaia replied. 'We were probably getting scared over nothing. I mean, apart from being unlucky if your building falls down when you are inside it, people aren't getting hurt just by going past the fallen down ones.'

'Yeah, you're right,' I said.

We said goodnight and walked off in opposite directions, back to our own homes.

Chapter Fifteen

That very night, I was watching the telly when they suddenly stopped the programme with a breaking news story. I had been eating my dinner. Tonight I'd made baked beans on toast and I was chasing the last two beans round my plate with my fork. However quickly or slowly I tried to shovel them up, I couldn't quite get them onto my fork. However hard I tried.

I was looking down at my plate when I heard the newsreader's voice. She sounded so anxious.

'We've just heard news of another devel-opment following the growing number of collapsing buildings in South London which, as yet, cannot be explained. Two council workers were discovered dead at one of the sites earlier tonight. Both men were examining the remnants of an abandoned warehouse, which collapsed only two nights ago. We are going live to Bill Franklin, who is at the scene.'

The screen flashed to a man standing in front of the debris of a fallen building. It was the one Gaia and I had been standing in front of only a few hours ago.

I dropped my fork and it made a loud clanging sound as it hit my plate.

'Thanks, Kathy. I'm standing just across the street from where the two council workers were discovered at about seven o'clock this evening. They have been identified as Richard Leighton and Frank Stewart. Both men were examining the rubble left when the warehouse collapsed, and the alarm was raised when neither man returned home earlier this evening. We do not know what went on here tonight, but the police have cordoned off this entire area, as you can see behind me. Their deaths are being treated as suspicious.'

Two large photos of the men filled the screen. They were both smiling. One of them had laughter lines round his eyes and rosy red cheeks. The other looked younger and had pale skin and light yellow hair.

I recognized them straight away.

They were the men in the yellow hard hats Gaia and I had walked past earlier that day.

Chapter Sixteen

The news went on and on about the two men all night. Suddenly the danger was greater. These two men hadn't been in a collapsed building; they'd died because of something else. Some people were saying that this might not have anything to do with what had happened with the buildings, that it could just be a coincidence that they'd died where a building had fallen. Until they'd done something called a post mortem, no one would know anything for sure.

That didn't stop them from talking about it, though.

I didn't put the lights on, so the room was lit up by the television. I stayed up late watching it even though there wasn't anything they could really tell us; they just kept saying the same kind of things over and over.

It was the same as with the buildings.

No one could explain why it was happening.

Chapter Seventeen

I went to find Gaia as soon as I got to school the next morning. She was sitting underneath the sunflowers. We had just a little time before they would blow the whistle to line up.

She looked tired, like she hadn't been to sleep much the night before.

'Gaia, did you see the news?' I said. 'Did you see what happened to those two men we saw?'

'Yes, I saw it,' she said, but she didn't say anything more.

'Why do you think they died?'

Gaia didn't say anything.

'Do you think . . . do you think that when we walked past again and didn't see them, they were . . .' My voice trailed off.

Fat tears rolled down Gaia's face. Her eyes looked large and glassy.

'What's wrong, Gaia?' I said. 'Are you upset about the men we saw? Don't worry.'

But whatever I said, she couldn't stop the tears from rolling down her face. They ran all the way down her cheeks and down her chin, making wet lines on her face until she pulled down her sleeve and wiped them away.

'It's OK, Gaia, it's OK.'

The whistle went and Gaia sniffed and wiped her face with her sleeve again.

'We shouldn't have gone out last night,' she said. 'It could have been us.' She slowly stood up and we walked into line.

We filed into school and sat down at our desks but there was no work on our tables to do. Usually we start the day answering maths questions but the board was blank and our books weren't out. Miss Farraway sat down on her chair and looked at us blankly, as if she couldn't remember why she was here, or why we were there either, for that matter.

'Miss Farraway,' said Paul. 'We haven't got our maths books.'

'Oh, yes,' said Miss Farraway. 'Maths books.'

'And there aren't any questions on the board,' Paul continued.

'Well,' said Miss Farraway, and it seemed like she was going to say something else after that, but she didn't. And she didn't make a move to get our books either.

'Miss Farraway, are you all right?' asked Olu, who's the kind of person who always looks after people who fall over in the playground and takes them upstairs for a plaster or an ice pack.

'Yes,' said Miss Farraway, but her eyes filled with tears.

'Miss Farraway!' said Olu and jumped out of her chair to comfort her.

'Thank you, Olu. I'm OK. Thank you. Sit down, lovely.'

But then she really started sobbing. No one knew what to do or what to say. This never happened. Teachers don't cry. Or if they do, they never do in front of us kids.

Olu stood paralysed halfway between Miss Farraway and her chair. Some of the girls started to cry a little bit themselves, although I wondered if they knew why.

I looked over to Gaia, who was looking down at her table, concentrating on a tiny spot on her desk.

Miss Farraway left the room in the end. She

just walked straight out. Miss Arnold, the deputy head, came in a few minutes later and found us some maths questions to do but we were all too stunned to do any of them.

'Is Miss Farraway OK, Miss Arnold?' Olu asked.

'She's very upset, as you have all seen. It's been a very upsetting time for lots of people at the moment. How are you all feeling with what's been going on?'

'I'm scared,' said someone straight away. I turned round and I saw the voice had come from Michael.

'Me too,' a few people agreed.

'I worry every night that our block will collapse,' said Paul. 'I can't sleep because of it.'

'I'm frightened about being outside,' said Olu.

'I'm scared something will happen to my little sister and my mum when they're at home during the day,' said Martha. 'What if I come home from school and our building's collapsed? What would I do?'

We went round and round, talking about our fears and worries. Miss Arnold never said that we shouldn't worry or that we'd be OK or anything like that. She just smiled sadly as someone else started speaking.

Gaia and I didn't say anything.

I listened to the sound of everyone's voices. They sounded high and coiled, as though they'd been wound up tighter and tighter until they were taut and could break any moment. I didn't want to hear their words any longer. I could feel my chest folding in on itself, smaller and smaller, as though it was trying to fit into a small square box, and my breaths came quickly and shallow. I felt like I couldn't breathe.

I heard someone say my name, and when I looked up Miss Arnold was standing over me and she'd put her hand on my shoulder.

'Are you all right, Ade?' she said.

I nodded, but she didn't stop looking away from me with the same worried eyes and I wished I could have told her the truth, right then. I wished I could have cried like some of the others and have Miss Arnold pat my back comfortingly. I wished I could have told her that I was scared.

Just like everyone else.

Chapter Eighteen

We had PE outside and threw brightly coloured balls to each other, standing in long lines across the playground. Gaia said that she had a stomach ache so she sat on the wall watching us. She kept pulling her sleeves down so they came over her wrists and her hands and then wrapping her arms around her like she was cold, even though it was another hot, sunny, airless day.

By lunch time she seemed to be feeling a little better. She ate a couple of mouthfuls from her plate, chewing steadily and staring into the distance, and then she turned to me suddenly and said, 'So, what do you think they're going to do now those men have died?'

'I don't know. They don't know how they died. I watched the news all night. They just said the same thing again and again. That their deaths were being treated as suspicious.'

'I don't think someone killed them,' Gaia said.

I looked at her questioningly.

'If no one killed them, how did they die?'

'I think,' Gaia continued, and she lowered her voice to a whisper, 'I think it had something to do with the buildings.'

'The buildings?'

'We had a bad feeling about them for a reason. I think there's something wrong with them,' she said.

'But how could a fallen-down building kill two men just by them standing next to it?'

'I don't know what's wrong with them, Adeola. I'm just saying I think they're something to do with it.'

Gaia looked cross for a moment. Then her face changed. She looked very worried.

'And I definitely don't think we should get close to them again,' she said. 'You won't, will you – go close to one again? I can always bring you some food from my house so you don't have to go to the shops.'

I knew what Gaia meant about having a bad feeling about the fallen buildings, but then we'd walked past them last night and we were fine now, so I wasn't sure she was right.

'Ade? Do you promise me? Don't go any-where near them.'

'OK,' I said.

It seemed better to agree with her than to make her panic. I didn't let on that I'd forgotten to get any milk last night and what we had left in the fridge had gone lumpy and sour-smelling. I just wouldn't tell her that I was going back to the shops tonight.

That way, I wouldn't worry her.

That evening there were lots and lots of policemen on the street. Some of them were standing in a line in front of the fallen buildings and others were walking around, with large, pointy-nosed Alsatians that were sniffing the pavements and the walls.

I decided to go to the closest newsagent, which was only a little shop but which had a fridge with pints of cold milk in it. It wasn't very far away. I had to go the same route as I had taken with Gaia the day before but I didn't stop to look at the buildings at all today. I hurried past the line of policemen that surrounded the area where the two men had been found. Finally I made it into the shop and bought a large bottle of milk so it would last us a bit longer.

'Be careful out there, sonny,' the shopkeeper said as he passed me my change. He looked out of the window as though he expected something to happen any moment. The bottle felt cold in my hands but I didn't wait for a bag. I wanted to get home as quickly as I could. Now that I was out on the streets, I was starting to feel more and more like Gaia was right, that I shouldn't have come out. I don't know if it was because of what Gaia had told me or if there really was something in the air, something menacing out there that said, *No one is safe.*

I decided I would run back to my tower. I could almost picture in my head exactly what was going to happen in the next few minutes. I would run down the road, turn off down the first street and sprint past the policemen and then run in a straight line to my tower, open the door and bang it behind me.

The door would go, *Slam!* No problems. I'd be safe.

Chapter Nineteen

I started running as soon as I left the shop. The bottle of milk felt heavy in my hands, so I had to hold it like a baby and it made me slow down a bit.

I turned down the street towards the policemen with one eye on my tower block in the distance. I wished I had never left it.

I ran past the policemen. The bored one, the one who yawned, the one who looked like he wanted to go home and have his dinner.

Then, suddenly, there was a shout.

I stopped and turned back in surprise.

Then I wished I had just carried on running.

One of the policemen I had just passed had fallen over. The policemen on either side of him were trying to help him up, but then, as they kneeled down to help him, they fell to the ground too. It was as if they had all suddenly fallen asleep.

Their helmets made a cracking sound as they hit the ground. *Crack, crack, crack.* One after the other.

I remember thinking it looked like a line of dominoes falling over, each one pushing the next one over in a line that was coming towards me.

I didn't know what to do. It's all so strange when you only have a split second to decide. It seems impossible that you are able to think of so many things at once in your head. Part of me thought I should be helping them. Another part thought I would be falling asleep and falling to the ground next, and then another part, the loudest of all, was thinking of Gaia.

Gaia's face, shouting, 'Run!'

That is what I did.

I dropped the milk and it exploded on the ground and I ran away as fast as I could.

I ran into my tower and I ran up the stairs and I didn't stop running even when I reached my corridor. I ran into my flat and slammed the front door behind me, and I only stopped when I was in my bedroom and the door was closed behind me.

I didn't have anywhere left to go.

It took a long time for my breathing to slow down. I don't really know if it was from the running or what I had just seen.

What had happened to those policemen? Why had they passed out like that? And the question I couldn't stop asking myself: had they just fallen asleep or was it something a lot more serious than that?

Had they died?

It was on the news that night.

A group of policemen had been found dead. Close to where the two council workers had been found. Their deaths were also being treated as suspicious.

Chapter Twenty

Suddenly there were lots of people who arrived in big white vans with satellites on top. People got quite excited in school when we found out that these were TV people.

We watched them through the bars of the playground gate. They had large black cameras perched on their shoulders like parrots. The newsreaders looked serious and worried one minute, when the camera was in front of them, and then laughed and smoked cigarettes the next. Some of them even came over and started filming the outside of our school.

I ran away to the other side of the playground when they did that and went to find Gaia. She was not hanging around the cameras either. She was sitting under the sunflowers picking up tiny little stones from the ground.

I sat beside her.

'Gaia, last night—' I started, but then I stopped myself. I didn't really want to tell her that I hadn't listened to her, but I had to tell someone about what I had seen.

'Last night, I saw what happened.'

'What do you mean?'

'I saw what happened to those policemen.'

'From your window?'

'No, I was there. I was standing next to them when it happened.'

Gaia lifted her head and looked me straight in the eye.

'I'd forgotten to get milk so I went really quickly to get some and then I was running past the policemen and they started falling over. One after the other. Just like they were falling asleep or something. I ran away when they started doing it. I didn't know that they were dying, I didn't know. They looked like they were just falling asleep.'

'Did they look like they were in pain?' Gaia asked.

'No, not really. They just fell down. It happened pretty quickly.'

Gaia didn't say anything. It looked like she was thinking it through.

'What do you think made them die?' I asked her.

'I've no idea,' she said. 'I still think it's to do with the fallen buildings, though. The policemen were right by one of them, weren't they?'

'Yes, the same one as those other two men. But they were standing just in front of it.'

'Have you looked out of your window recently? Have you seen how the buildings are falling?'

'What do you mean?'

'There's a pattern,' Gaia said.

She reached into her pocket and brought out a folded-up piece of paper and handed it to me.

It was a drawing but it took me a moment to realize it was a map. A map of where we lived. There was a drawing of Gaia's tower and my block and our school. Then there were lots of red dots which had numbers next to them. They roughly made a circle shape. In the middle of the circle was a star that was labelled *Pub – The George,* which had a number one written next to it.

'I've been filling it in each night. The red dots are the fallen buildings. And the numbers show the day they fell in. It's how many days have

92

passed since that first pub fell down. Can you see how it's spreading outwards? The number twos and threes are close to the pub and then the nines and tens are on the outside.'

'What's this one here?' I pointed to a red dot that looked like it had a one and a two next to it.

'That's twelve. Twelve days after. It looks like the buildings which have been missed out are falling now.'

'And these are our blocks,' I said, pointing to the two wobbly drawings of our towers, one with a capital G above it and the other with a capital A.

'Yes,' Gaia said.

'They're so close to the other fallen build-ings.' Our towers were right next to buildings which had fallen five days after the pub collapsed. 'It . . . it . . . could be us next.'

'Yes. Exactly,' Gaia said.

'Have you shown this to anyone?' I said.

Gaia shrugged.

'I wonder if the police have realized this is happening,' I said.

'I'm sure they know,' Gaia said. 'Maybe they're hiding it from us so we don't all panic.'

'What do you mean?'

'Well, I was talking to Mum about it last night and she wants us to pack up and leave now.'

'Leave?' My voice sounded sharp and shaky all at the same time. 'Where would you go?'

'She wants to go to my aunt's. She lives in Brighton. My mum said we should get out while we can.'

'Brighton? Where's that?'

'It's south. Down by the sea. I went there once when I was little.'

'Are you going then?'

'My dad doesn't want us to go.'

'Oh. So are you going to stay?'

'I guess so. Dad usually gets his own way. Has your mum spoken to you about it?'

'No. I'm not sure how much she knows about what's going on, to be honest. I guess I'm staying too. Here you go,' I said, handing back the map.

'You can have it, if you like. We can both fill it in. You can give it back to me tomorrow.'

'OK,' I said and I put the map in my pocket.

Neither of us could have known that we would not see each other tomorrow. Or the day after that. Or the day after that.

The very next day, they closed our school.

Chapter Twenty-one

Most people were leaving.

I could see them going from my window.

There was a steady procession of people out on the pavements. They were carrying as much as they could, in brightly coloured bags, or dragging large suitcases behind them. All their belongings in the world.

I spent a long time checking through the line of people to see if I could see Gaia and her family among them.

I wondered if her dad had changed his mind and they were on their way to Brighton, right now, to her aunt's house.

Or if her parents were fighting. Not able to agree over what they were going to do and Gaia and her brothers trying not to hear the shouting through the thin walls.

I had no way of telling. We didn't have a

phone at my house. Mum had a mobile but I didn't know where she kept it.

I felt in my pocket for the map that Gaia had given me, and traced the numbered dots with my finger until I came to rest upon Gaia's drawing of her block. I missed her.

I tried to shake the thought from my head that I might never see her again but it kept returning over and over in my mind, making me feel sick and panicky. The only thing that calmed me was turning over the map that Gaia had made in my hands. It was my last piece of her. I didn't have any photographs, only the pictures in my head and the worn paper map I was holding.

I hoped that she had got out. I hoped that she had left her flat behind her and was far away from the piles of brick and rubble that made up our streets now. No one was safe in their homes any more. Bricks and walls and doors didn't protect you any longer.

Perhaps she was already there. In Brighton. Down by the sea. I'd only seen the sea once when we went on a trip to the beach in Year Two and it had scared me a bit. It was so vast, so unending, stretching on and on until it met the sky. Gaia had held my hand as we waded into the shallow waters because I told her I was afraid, and she'd squeezed it tight as the first wave rolled in and splashed us right up to our waists. I screamed, I think, but I didn't feel as worried with Gaia beside me.

I wished I was with Gaia again. Perhaps I could have gone with her family to Brighton and escaped as well.

I knew it was a good idea to get out, but the problem was, I just couldn't go anywhere without Mum.

Chapter Twenty-two

Michael's mum came round a couple of days after our school shut and told me to pack up my things.

She marched into Mum's bedroom and started shouting at her to get up. To save her son. To save herself. Mum looked right through Michael's mum as if she hadn't just been screamed at, and turned over on her side to go back to sleep.

Michael's mum grabbed my wrist then and started half yelling at me. She said that I would go with them, that I would be safe then. She told me to pack some of my clothes, that she'd be back soon.

I closed the door behind her and locked it with the big key that we hardly ever use. I put the chain on as well. Then I pushed my chest of drawers in front of the door. It was too heavy for me to lift, so I had to move one side forward and then the other. It took me a while to move it like this, in little zigzags, but I got it there in the end. Just before Michael's mum came back.

She really started yelling when she realized I wasn't going to open the door. Even louder than she did at Mum. *Ade, Ade, Ade.* She kept saying my name over and over. I even heard Michael's sister shouting my name. But it didn't last for ever. And then I heard their footsteps fade away. They had left too.

I went out to buy some food from the shops after that. I knew it was dangerous but we were running out again and we had to eat.

I walked out of my tower, but before I turned towards the shops, I looked down the road to where Gaia's block was standing. Was she still in there? I counted the windows up until I found the seventeenth floor and tried to see through the dark panes.

Maybe she was looking at me at this very same moment that I was looking towards her?

Just in case she was, I put my hand up and waved a little bit. Then I started to feel silly, so I stopped and started running down the road to the shop.

The one closest to us was closed, with the grey shutters pulled right down, so I had to go to a mini supermarket that was down the road.

There was no one else in the supermarket when I went round filling my basket and there were lots of things missing from the shelves. I decided to buy some chocolate biscuits as a treat, the type that are filled with white marshmallow, and remembered to get some toilet roll for us too.

The man who served me was very tall and looked quite nervous. He kept looking around us as if he thought that someone was going to jump out from behind the shelves at any minute. I filled up a couple of plastic bags and their handles dug into my hands, cutting bright pink lines into my skin. I'd only gone a few steps down the road when I saw that the sign on the door had been changed to CLOSED.

I'd only just got there in time.

The street was deserted, and all of a sudden I felt very alone. There weren't many cars or buses on the roads either, which is very odd because usually the main road has a big traffic jam on it. People around here say it is the only thing you can really depend upon. You never know if the sun is going to shine or if the day is going to go your way but you know there'll be a traffic jam, bumper to bumper, on the main road.

I didn't like the empty-looking street.

I didn't realize how much I liked the busy-ness of everything and how, without it, I felt more lonely. The bags of shopping were too heavy for me to be able to run, and walking felt slow and tiring. It made me play a secret game which I have never told anyone about, not even Gaia.

I imagine that I see an animal wandering behind me on the street.

Maybe it is hiding behind a dustbin or creeping round the corner. It could be any animal. I've had elephants, giraffes, horses and even rabbits in the past, although usually it is a dog or a cat. Sometimes the same one comes up, without me even thinking about it. There's a black-and-white dog that often turns up, and a small tabby kitten that I've seen a few times.

I imagine that the animal is following me home, so every time I look round, I can see it there behind me. By the time I get back to my block, it comes up right next to me so it's by my side, and then we walk up the stairs together to my flat. I always take the stairs on those days because it's fun to imagine them running up in front of me and then waiting for me to catch up with them. Or balancing on the banister and then leaping down in front of me.

And I don't think animals like the lift. It makes them feel like they are trapped.

Then, when we get back to my flat, I feed them their favourite food. I make this part up too, of course. I don't put down real food or anything like that. Then I make them a bed for the night and that's it.

I guess they are imaginary friends of sorts and that's why I don't tell anyone about them, because I don't want people to think I am weird. I don't talk to them or anything, other than in the normal way you might talk to any animal, like, 'Here boy!' or, 'It's OK, don't be scared,' or, 'I won't hurt you,' but actually I do all the talking in my head, otherwise Mum might hear me and I'd wake her. The animals don't really have names either.

And the other thing is that they are always gone in the morning. The first time it happened, I spent a long time looking for the creature everywhere, even under the bed and in the kitchen cupboards, just in case it got trapped or was lost somewhere, but it was nowhere to be found. I still spend a while looking for them in the morning each time, just in case. Perhaps one day, it'll still be there when I wake up and I won't feel that stab of sadness that I'm alone again.

That day, it was the black-and-white dog who strolled towards me, and because he knows me now, he gave my hand a lick and looked at me in that loving way dogs do. I was glad to see him. I gently stroked him from his eyes right to the back of his head, just the way he likes. As we walked together, he stuck close to me and I put my shopping bags into one hand and kept my other hand by my side, so I could feel his soft fur as we made our way back to the tower.

We didn't meet anyone else on the way. At one point, he sniffed the air as if he could smell something, but then he carried on walking and soon enough we were back at my tower. We climbed the stairs to my flat, the dog bounding a few steps ahead of me all the way and then turning every once in a while to see where I was.

He slept at the bottom of my bed that night. I fell asleep more easily than I had done in a while with him there, and when I woke in the early morning, when it was still dark outside, he was still there, sleeping in the tight circle his body made.

But when I woke in the morning, with the sun streaming through my curtains, he'd gone. I thought I could see the indent his body had made in my duvet, which felt warm to touch, so maybe he'd only just left.

I didn't spend as long looking for him this time. I knew in my heart that I was alone once more.

Chapter Twenty-three

I've already told you about the TV crews that arrived, haven't I? Well, lots more came after they closed my school.

It was funny seeing streets that I know on the television. They didn't look right. They looked greyer and darker and smaller somehow.

Sometimes they interviewed people who lived nearby and they talked about how scared they were and they often said that they were packing up and leaving their homes.

'You aren't safe inside your home and you aren't safe on the streets any more. There's nowhere left to go,' I remember one woman saying. She had a baby sitting on her hip the whole time she was talking, playing with her hair.

I always wondered if Gaia or her mum might suddenly appear on the television. Maybe they would tell me that they were leaving, so I would know for sure that they had gone and that Gaia would be safe.

I would always run back to the television if I could hear different voices other than the serious tones of the newsreaders to see if it was them. But they never turned up.

I spent a lot of time watching television because there wasn't much else to do. Sometimes I dreamed I could hear Michael's mum calling for me to walk to school and I would wake up with a start and think I needed to rush out, before I remembered that Michael's mum had gone now and that school didn't exist any more.

It's funny because sometimes when I was at school, especially if we had tests or long pieces of writing to do, I used to wish I was back at home, watching television and not doing anything much at all. Now that I was at home watching television all day, I wished I was back at school. I missed Miss Farraway and how our classroom was always warm and colourful. I missed listening to stories read aloud to us. I missed seeing Gaia every day.

My head sometimes hurt for no reason and I wished I could run outside and feel the air rushing by my cheeks as I ran but I didn't dare leave the tower unless I really needed to. I felt foggy some days and nothing seemed to make me feel much better. I just carried on watching television, even if I had a headache, because at least that way I could hear people speaking.

One day I was watching television and they started talking about 'the Blucher Disaster'. Blucher is the name of the road which Gaia and I walked down, the one where the first two men and the policemen who had died were found.

They were talking about everything that had been happening and whether or not the army should be sent in. The problem was that they didn't know what they were fighting, so it was all well and good to send the army in but they didn't know who or what the enemy was.

The people talking on the programme were getting very red-faced and blustery when not everyone agreed with what they were saying. Then they started talking to another man through a video link. He had large pink cheeks that wobbled when he spoke.

'Prime Minister, what is being done to help the people affected by the Blucher Disaster?' they asked him. 'It seems like not a lot from where we are sitting.'

'No, that's not true,' he started, and then he was speaking a lot of words but they weren't making any sense at all. I don't know how else to explain it. He was talking a lot but it was like it didn't really mean anything.

I knew a little bit about the Prime Minister but I couldn't really believe that it was this man, with his pink, jowly cheeks and nervous, dashing eyes, who was in charge of our country. I couldn't stop thinking that he didn't have any idea what to say, that he didn't know what to do, and if the Prime Minister didn't know what to do then what hope was there?

I didn't watch it for long and I changed the channel to someone talking about the number of people who had died so far, and there were people who knew them, their families, crying and talking about how much they missed them.

I turned the television off for a while after that.

The funny thing about the programme which had the Prime Minister on was that after that, everyone started calling the whole thing the Blucher Disaster. People pronounced it wrong sometimes and said things like 'Bloosher' or 'Bloocher', but soon enough, everyone was saying it right, and made that funny little 'uh' sound that comes in the middle of words like book and look before the 'ch'. Bl-uh-ch-er. You know you are saying it right when it sounds like something that would knock you round the head.

One minute, we weren't calling it that, and the next, it had caught on so much that in the end, people were using it to describe anything horrible that was happening.

When a building collapsed and fell down on a group of teenagers, it was all part of the Blucher Disaster.

When a woman was found collapsed dead with her bag of shopping spilling onto the road, it was the Blucher Disaster.

It was all the same to them. And in the end, I guess they were right.

This was how the plants first got their name. Bluchers. Someone called them that once on TV and it stuck.

Chapter Twenty-four

No one knew about the Bluchers for what seemed like a long time.

There were all kinds of reasons and ideas about why our buildings were falling down and why people were collapsing. After what happened to the two men and the policemen, people were being attacked every day.

It was a horrible, horrible time.

I could see from my window if there was a little blob of a person who was not moving. Then I would see an ambulance arrive and people in brightly coloured jackets would swarm around the body and carry it away.

I hadn't left our flat for a really long time since school had shut down. I got into a rhythm each day which revolved around food, looking out of the window and television. The first thing I would do when I got up was to make breakfast for Mum and me and tidy up anything from the night before. I'd take Mum's plate into her bedroom and leave it on her bedside table because she'd always be asleep. Then I'd watch the morning news for a few hours and find out anything new that had happened.

One day, I thought I'd switch on the news and they'd say that they'd found a way to make it safe for everybody again. It had to happen sooner or later, didn't it?

After that, I would sit and look out of the window. From where I sat, I could see the little holes left by fallen buildings, as if someone had come along and taken bites of brick and concrete here and there. I'd spend some time updating Gaia's map with any more buildings that had fallen. There were more and more dots to make each day.

I'd make lunch next. Something simple like crackers and cheese or a tin of soup. Then more television and window-watching before dinner.

It always felt like I was waiting for something to happen, whether it was for someone to make everything safe once more or something as simple as seeing Mum awake. I would be sitting watching television and then I would hear the sound of the door handle squeaking from her bedroom. I tried to stop myself from running up to her and asking her a hundred questions and giving her a hug, and instead I would just sit where I was, in front of the television.

I ran up to her like that once before, and she didn't like it.

I sprang up as soon as I heard the door opening. 'Mum!' I said. 'I'm home all the time now. They closed the school down because it's not safe any more. There's lots of people leaving. Do you think we should go? We'd have to be careful because there's something that's making you fall over and die . . .'

I was excited, I hadn't spoken to anyone since the day Michael's mum had tried to take me with her and I'd been to the shop for some food. That tall, nervous-looking man who served me in the shop was the last person I had spoken to. It had been six days.

Mum was saying something under her breath which stopped my flow of words.

'Stop, stop, stop,' she was saying.

She turned towards the bathroom and shot me the same look she'd given me the day I asked her to come shopping with me. Her eyes looked small and weren't open properly, as if all the sleeping was making her eyelids stick together. But I could still see what they were saying: *Stop talking. It's hurting me.*

She went to the bathroom and I heard the sound of the toilet flushing and then she went back inside her bedroom.

I knew better after that. I stayed still if I heard her come out. I might have turned my head towards her and sometimes she might have given me a little nod, but that was all.

I really missed being able to talk to Gaia. Especially with everything that was happening. I wished I could have talked to her about it and heard what she thought. Did she still think that the fallen-down buildings had something to do with the collapsing people? Did she think it was funny, like me, that they were using the name of Blucher Road in all the news reports now? Didn't she think it was actually quite a threatening-sounding word if you said it over and over to yourself?

I just had to have these conversations in my head and imagine what Gaia might say. It wasn't the same as actually speaking to her, but it helped a little. Sometimes I would even replay old conversations we'd had in my head.

'You know what I heard on the radio this morning?' Gaia had said to me one day when we were sitting in the playground. 'These scientists were doing a test with plants to see if they treated their sibling plants differently to stranger plants.'

'Oh,' I said.

'Guess what they found.'

'That they don't treat them any differently. They're plants.'

'No! They found that they did! They were less aggressive towards their sibling plants. They don't take up as much root space, so their sibling's got room to grow too. Isn't that amazing?'

'But how do they know which plant is their sibling?'

'The scientists don't know how they do it. They don't know how they recognize them.'

'That's weird.'

'It's incredible. We really only know such a tiny amount about how plants behave.'

'Yeah, I guess so.'

Gaia used to present me with these little nuggets of information that she picked up all the time. It was always something interesting that I hadn't considered or realized or heard about, and quite often it was to do with plants because she loved them so much. I missed hearing her telling me something amazing she had just discovered about the world. Gaia had made me realize what a wonderful and strange place we lived in.

I kept filling in the map that she had given me. It was my way of feeling close to her, I suppose. Each day I drew in more and more numbered red dots. I was running out of space now. There were so many red dots close to each other, it was beginning to look entirely red.

I found myself missing Gaia a little bit more on the days when something new happened. I wanted to be able to talk it through with her. Otherwise it didn't feel like it was real, like it was actually happening.

One of those days was when the news kept showing the same thing on every channel. A woman with curly blonde hair was talking. Her face filled most of the screen, so I could see that she had little lines round her mouth where her face would crease when she smiled. But she wasn't smiling then. She had made a discovery about what was killing those people. She'd found something in their throats. It was so, so small that we would not be able to see it if we only used our eyes. She had discovered them using a special microscope.

She called them spores.

I didn't know what spores were or where they came from but I was glad that I saw that lady on the news. She said it was best to stay indoors if you could and avoid going outside. I hoped Gaia knew about the spores so that, if she was still in her tower, she would know how dangerous it was to go out. Mum and I were going to be out of food again soon, so I had been planning to go to the shops, but I wasn't going to leave the tower now.

In the end, I decided to knock on a neighbour's door to see if they had any food. I hadn't left our flat in a good few days now and as I opened the front door, I started to feel nervous about stepping out of it.

This is what Mum must feel like, I thought.

The corridor was completely empty. I couldn't hear a sound apart from the tread of my own footsteps. I crept out of my flat, looking all around me as if something was going to jump out at me.

The first door I came to was Michael's mum's flat, although I knew that they had gone, so there was no point in knocking. As I walked past it, though, I could see the door had been left ajar by just a few inches.

I gingerly pushed the door open and it swung wide, revealing the deserted flat.

'Hello?' I said, although I knew there wasn't anyone there.

Inside, the flat looked like it had been turned upside down and shaken really hard. Clothes were strewn across the floor, books had been flung off the shelves. Cupboard doors were left gaping open, waiting to be closed. A lamp in the sitting room stood illuminating the chaos. I walked towards it and switched it off.

I went into the kitchen and plucked a couple of cans of beans and a bag of rice from the first cupboard I came to. I told myself that I'd make a list of everything I took, so that if things ever got back to normal, we could replace it all when Michael and his family came home.

I hurried back to my flat then, putting the cans and the rice into a sling I made with the front of my T-shirt.

I left the door ajar, just as I'd found it.

Perhaps they had left in a real rush and forgot to pull the door closed to lock it. I'd never seen it left open before.

Or, a voice in my head said, *perhaps Michael's mum left their flat open on purpose, so I could take their food if I needed it.*

I'd never know, but I had a feeling in my belly that she did leave it open for me.

Chapter Twenty-five

I watched so much television during this time that after a while I realized I wasn't really watching it any more. It was just noise that was making my head sore. Gaia used to say that too much television was bad for you, so now and again I switched it off and tried to do something else.

Sometimes I would play this little game that I made up, called Five in the House. I had to clear a space on our table to play it.

I had collected lots and lots of little yogurt pots which I kept in a box under my bed. They all looked exactly the same because I had taken the labels off and I'd washed them so they didn't smell or anything.

I'd put out loads and loads of yogurt pots upside down on the table, until it was completely covered with them.

It looked like a little city.

Then I would screw up five bits of paper, so I'd have five little paper balls, and I'd hide them under the yogurt pots. Sometimes I would put just one ball under five pots. Other times I might put three under one pot and two under another. I could do it any way I liked.

When I'd done that, I would move the yogurt pots round and round, so they were all mixed up. There was no way I could tell where I'd put the paper balls because I'd mix them up for a really long time.

The object of the game was to lift up the right pots to find all five balls, to find five in a house. I would let myself have ten chances to find them.

It was quite hard and I'd only managed to do it a handful of times, but I liked it because it took quite a long time to play it. It always took me a while to choose which ten yogurt pots I would lift up.

The other thing I spent my time doing was filling in my scrapbook.

Before, when I'd been able to go outside, I had cut out pictures from old newspapers I'd found on the street to stick into my scrapbook. But now I had to copy out pictures and words that I'd heard from the television instead.

The pages were filling up.

I sometimes look back to the page where I first wrote down their name.

They are called BLUCHERS.

It took us a long time to find them.

I'd filled loads of pages with all the terrible things that had been happening before we found out about the Bluchers.

It was just after they found out about the spores, when they first saw them. I was playing Five in the House, so I'd switched the television off for a bit. When I turned it back on, the first thing I saw was a Blucher, filling the screen.

Of course, I had no idea what it was at that moment, so my first thought was that it looked quite beautiful. It was shiny and had a bit on the top that was shaped like a sunflower seed, with the tip pointing upwards. Except that it was more like a ball; it wasn't flat. It was about as big as one of my fists, I suppose, with a little stalk holding the top part up.

What made me think it was beautiful was its colour. It was almost blue and almost silver. Not like any colour that I could make up with paint or pencils, anyway. I couldn't make my picture of that Blucher look very much like it at all.

And the funny thing was that the colour seemed to be moving.

It wasn't changing colour exactly, but the colour was moving. It's the best way I can describe it.

'These images are coming live from the Blucher Disaster area,' the newsreader was saying, 'where this plant has just been discovered. Its origin has not been identified and scientists have already confirmed that this is a completely new species.' I guess because they had a little stalk and a bit on top, they were first called a type of plant. Although really they weren't anything like a plant. They looked like nothing else I had ever seen.

When I realized what it was I was looking at, I could see its beauty dissolve before my eyes. The blue-silver colour reminded me of knives, of grey clouds before a thunderstorm. The way the colour moved and shifted made me think of a predator stalking its prey, silently pacing towards it before it goes in for the kill.

Bluchers weren't beautiful at all. They were evil, menacing, deadly.

After the first sighting of the Bluchers, they started to pop up more and more.

Soon, I was able to see clusters from my window. What started out as little patches of silvery-blue soon spread out and covered the ground below me. They grew so fast that sometimes it seemed the patches were swelling in front of my eyes.

Now they had lots of people on the television who knew about plants and fungi.

I wasn't able to follow most of it. I caught certain words like *fruiting body* and *chemical trails*, which I wrote down in my book, but I didn't understand how the Bluchers worked.

The only thing I truly grasped was that they thought they knew why the buildings were falling down. It was because of the Bluchers. Gaia had been right all along. The falling buildings and the people collapsing on the street were linked. They were both being caused by the Bluchers.

Not only were they sending out deadly spores into the air; they were feeding on concrete and stone and glass and metal. They released some kind of wet stuff which could dissolve all those kind of things. That had a special name too. Enim or enzim, or something like that.

Bluchers.

The word sat heavily on my chest. Whenever I closed my eyes I could see their shiny silvery heads leering towards me. I could sense their hunger, urgently and desperately feeding upon the buildings that were our homes. And when I opened my eyes again, I could see that we were surrounded by them.

When I first learned that the Bluchers fed on buildings, I went to lie next to Mum for a bit. I started to go over everything that I had heard about them in my head. When I thought about it, it made me want to hold onto Mum tight. I didn't want to wake her, though, so I just put my head against her back and leaned into her a bit. She felt warm and solid and real against me.

I wished she would wake up.

I was afraid.

I guess I had always been a bit worried that our tower might fall down like all those other buildings. But I'd never really thought it would happen. Because our block was so tall I thought that it was too big to collapse underneath us. But if the Bluchers were eating buildings and were getting bigger all the time, then they could start feeding on the tower at any moment.

I forced myself to get up and look out of the window.

I hadn't looked out properly in the last day or so. I had been glued to the television or sleeping.

When I looked out that morning, I heard myself gasp out loud. As far as I could see, I saw the silvery-blue colour of the Bluchers.

The city was being flattened out.

We had used rolling pins once in class to roll out some clay, and it made me think of that. Like someone had taken a giant rolling pin and was evening all the buildings out.

There were still some standing. The other towers around me were still there. I had even seen some of their lights on a couple of nights ago.

One night I had counted up to Gaia's flat on her tower, to the seventeenth floor, and saw a light on. I told myself that it didn't mean she was definitely still living there. Perhaps they'd left the light on in their rush to leave. I remembered the way Michael's flat looked. They'd forgotten to turn a lamp off when they'd left.

But part of me couldn't stop thinking that she could still be in there, that her dad might not have let them leave, and if that was true, then they were trapped. Just like me and Mum.

I'd never been afraid of heights before, but as I looked down, the ground suddenly seemed much further away than before and I thought I felt the floor move beneath me. I had to sit down very still on a chair until I felt normal again. It was quite a while before I could stand.

I didn't know what to do.

It was too late to leave now because of the spores in the air that we could not see. And it was only a matter of time before the Bluchers would eat the tower and we would crash to the ground.

I wasn't going to be able to save myself and Mum. Not on my own, anyway.

We needed someone to rescue us.

I decided to ring the police.

They would come and get us out. They probably had some masks that they could wear over their faces that would stop spores getting into their mouths. And they would bring two extra ones for me and Mum too.

We don't have a phone in our flat but Mum had a mobile, although I wasn't sure where it was. In the end, after looking through a couple of bags and in a few drawers, I found it under a pile of unopened post on the side. Nothing happened. The battery was dead. I'd seen Mum using the charger but I didn't know where she kept it. I looked in all the drawers in the sitting room and the kitchen, and even in the little cupboard in the bathroom that has a mirror on it, but I couldn't find it. I realized it must have been in her bedroom.

The room was dark because she kept the curtains closed all the time. I tried to see if I could feel the charger on the floor with my hands, and then I tried to look in the wardrobe, but the door banged against something when I opened it and made a noise.

I heard Mum move in her bed. She didn't say anything but I gave up then. I didn't want to risk waking her up.

There wasn't a lot I could do, so I sat in front of the television for most of the day. Every channel had something on about the Bluchers. I wished they'd put something else on instead. I was sick of hearing about them. Maybe I should have switched it off but I wanted to hear people speaking, anything other than the voice in my head asking me how could we possibly survive this. In the end, I left it on all night and fell asleep on the sofa, in front of the lit-up screen.

The first thing I heard the next day was people talking in really loud, cross voices on the television. There were about eight people sitting on a stage and there was an audience in front of them.

People in the audience were asking questions about the Bluchers, and they kept clapping and cheering when someone on the stage answered them. I couldn't follow what they were talking about but they kept saying the same word over and over.

I wrote it down in my book so I didn't forget it.

Contaminayshon

I didn't know what it meant but it sounded bad. I changed the channel to the news. They were talking about how they'd tried to set fire to the Bluchers. They showed a film of a fireman with what looked like a water hose but when he pressed a button, a jet of fire came out of it. He covered a group of Bluchers in flames.

At first, you couldn't see them through the fire. It looked like they'd been burned out.

Then the smoke cleared and you could see that they weren't hurt by the fire at all.

Not one bit.

I wrote that down in my book too.

Chapter Twenty-six

The next morning when I woke up, everything seemed very quiet.

I lay in bed, unmoving, listening. There was nothing to hear.

I turned onto my side and my bed creaked loudly, disturbing the silence. It seemed to echo on after I'd moved.

I stood up slowly, very aware of every movement I made. I could hear the pad of my feet on the floor, the rasp as I scratched my head, the clash of my teeth as I swallowed.

Why could I not hear anything but the sounds I was making? Where was everyone else?

I was afraid to look out of the window, frightened of what I would see or what I wouldn't see, but I walked towards it in small steps and climbed up onto the ledge to look down at the streets below me. Except I couldn't really call them streets any more. You couldn't see where there had been roads now. The Bluchers had eaten through them all.

Everything was still. No buses or cars or ambulances whizzing around any more. No people walking. No little bicycles weaving in between everyone. Those things were all long gone now. Before, there had been helicopters flying over a lot, but that morning they weren't there. The sky was completely empty. I couldn't even see any planes flying past.

I'd stopped filling in Gaia's map days ago. There was not enough space for the red dots any more.

I didn't like the silence and went to switch the television on but the screen didn't flicker. I tried it again. Nothing.

I remembered that I had left it on last night again, when I went to sleep. It must have broken in the night. I tried switching it on and off at the wall but I couldn't make it work.

Without the voices from the television, I started to feel lonely. I knew Mum was there but she hadn't been talking to me a lot recently. I'd even started to think that she was waiting for me to go to sleep before she got up. The last few nights, I thought I had heard the sound of a door opening just as I was falling asleep.

I decided to add a new drawing to my notebook.

I drew the wide, empty sky and the deserted ground. It didn't take me long to finish it.

After that I thought I'd cook lunch early to give me something to do, but when I tried to turn the taps on, no water came out. Sometimes, our taps don't let out water straight away and then they give a sort of splutter before some comes out. That day, I couldn't even make it splutter. I turned the taps round and round so many times, I couldn't remember the right way to turn them on or off any more.

I tried the taps in the bathroom, but those ones weren't working either. I even went to Michael's flat and tried his taps too.

In our kitchen fridge, we had a little bit of milk left and a few cartons of orange juice, but that was all we had to drink.

I poured out a cupful of milk and took a gulp but it had soured and tasted horrible and it was all I could do not to spit it out on the floor. I made it to the sink just in time.

I emptied one of the cartons of orange juice

into a cup and then poured half into another cup. I tiptoed into Mum's room and left her half on the bedside table, and then I sat on the sofa trying to drink mine as carefully as I could.

Time went very slowly that day and I found myself wishing I was back at school again.

I played with some Lego for a while and I read through my notebook a few times but mostly it felt like I was waiting for something to happen.

I played a game that I used to play all the time, called Wink Murder. I'm not sure why I call it that because it's not the one that everyone plays when you sit in a big circle and someone winks at you and you pretend to die and make silly noises. And it's not about murder either. This one you can play by yourself.

You look out of the window and hold one finger up right in front of you. Then you close one eye and open the other and keep doing that, closing and opening one eye at a time. You'll see that your finger looks like it's moving from one side to the other, jumping back and forth.

The aim of the game is to try and line up your finger so that it jumps between two things. I used to do it between two buildings from my window.

When you can get it to jump from one thing to another thing, that means that you've got those ones and then you play again.

I didn't play it for long this time though.

It didn't seem like much fun any more.

There was a new kind of darkness that night. It was blacker, thicker and it happened a lot faster, like someone had quickly drawn a curtain on the day. I hadn't known a night like it. It took me a while to realize that the orange streetlights had not come on. In fact, I couldn't see any lights from my window, and there were no lights on in Gaia's tower either.

I went to switch the lights on in our flat but they didn't come on. I tried every light switch – even the one in Mum's room – but none of them worked. I tried them all again, just to be sure, running around frantically, desperately checking each one. But they wouldn't come on. There was nothing to break the black hold of the night.

I sat in the darkness, hugging my legs to myself and tucking my head in as well, as if I was a tortoise hiding in its shell. I started to shake. I couldn't stop myself. Not just part of me but my whole body, as if I was cold and trying to make myself warm again. I could feel my teeth rattling against each other and though I tried to stop, the shaking turned to tears which fell down my face and I heard myself make a sound like a moan. It wasn't unlike the sound that Mum had made the day I walked in to find her cut up and bruised.

I called out to Mum in the end, but she didn't answer me. My voice sounded small when I said her name, like someone had turned my volume down.

I tried to imagine that one of my animals might come and visit me. Perhaps an owl could have flown up to the window, a snowy white one with wings that spread open as wide as my arms, and I could let it in and feed it mice. But no animals came to me that night and I tried not to think about it too much because that had never happened before.

In the end, I pretended Gaia was next to me. I closed my eyes and summoned her face in front of me. I imagined her telling me something bizarre and wonderful she had just found out.

'Ade, did you know that there's a fungus that lives under the ground? It's really rather clever because it sort of joins onto tree roots and gives the root water that it needs to grow. And because the fungus helps the tree, the tree gives the fungus food so it can live. Cool, right?'

'Yes,' I replied, my head full of roots stretching out into a network.

'So they sort of help each other live by giving the other what they need.'

'Like they're friends?'

'Exactly, like they're friends!' she said, smiling.

Imagining Gaia helped me to just about drift off.

But when I did get to sleep, I kept waking up again, hoping it was morning, but it was still black outside each time I opened my eyes.

Every time I woke, it took me a long while to get back to sleep again.

I didn't think the night would ever end.

PART TWO

Now

Chapter Twenty-seven

So that's what's happened to me.

That's why I'm still here in the tower, surrounded by Bluchers. I wonder if there are other people trapped like us and I wonder why no one has come to rescue us yet. Like they do on television. If something bad happens to someone on television, somebody always comes along to rescue them.

But that doesn't happen here.

I've been watching the buildings falling. Sometimes it happens right in front of my eyes. I see the surge of the Bluchers, writhing around the base of a building, dissolving the brick, layer by layer. Then the walls start to lean just a fraction before it plummets to the ground. There's something slow and fast about the way a building falls. At first, it's so slow that it doesn't look like it's happening, and then suddenly it accelerates and collapses in one swooping, engulfing crash.

The other day I saw one of the smaller blocks fall, and just as it started to lean over on itself, I saw the door at the bottom of the block open and the tiny figure of someone dashing out. They ran in a diagonal line, desperately, in lunging strides, but in only a few steps they had collapsed from the spores. I could see the body lying unmoving on the ground. It looked like it was a woman with short, dark hair. She looked a bit like Miss Arnold but I don't know if it was her.

Then the Bluchers came, one by one, in a blue-silver haze. At first there were only a couple but as I watched, a group collected together, and for a moment they seemed to pause, as if they were waiting for something. Then they covered the body until I could see it no longer.

I think about Gaia a lot. I hope that she did escape and that she's safe. I imagine she's somewhere in the countryside. I don't know if that is what Brighton is like but I imagine it is in my head. Somewhere green where there are lots of trees and not many buildings, where there aren't any Bluchers around.

My mouth feels rough and dry from

sleeping. I divide up another orange juice carton and I sip at my half with tiny little mouthfuls but still I finish it quickly. It feels like I haven't drunk anything though; my mouth just feels sticky and orangey instead. I open another carton and pour out half, and this time I drink it how I want to, in big, loud gulps.

I brush my teeth afterwards. It's difficult without water. The toothpaste sticks to my teeth and they feel grainy afterwards but I like the minty taste. It makes me feel a bit better although my head is starting to hurt now. As if someone is trying to squeeze my brain like you squeeze a sponge. I think it's because I haven't had any water. Everyone knows that orange juice is OK but water is the best.

We learned about it in school when we grew the seeds. We all need water and if we don't get it, it's not good. We stopped giving water to some of the little sunflower plants when they were still quite small and they went all floppy, like they couldn't stand up properly.

I go to my bedroom to see if I can find my school bag. It's been pushed under my bed, forgotten about, but I find it in the end and pull out my topics book. I turn the pages to the one that was about the time the sunflowers went floppy and see the word I'm looking for.

It comes back to me now.

'They are dehydrated,' said Miss Farraway. 'That means that they have not got enough water. What are they?'

'Dehydrated,' we chanted back to her.

This is how I feel: floppy and tired and my legs don't want to hold me up. I cut out the word from the worksheet. It's in large black letters and I stick it into my scrapbook.

I have DEHYDRATION

I end up falling asleep, which is funny because I couldn't sleep properly at night and now it is daytime and I can't stay awake. But when I wake up I feel worse, not better.

It is weird because you usually feel better when you've had a sleep. Mum used to tell me that I was full of beans whenever I woke up from a nap. But I don't feel like that now. My head hurts more and my tongue feels too big in my mouth. It's hard to swallow.

I start thinking about our last carton of juice in the fridge. More than anything, I want to drink it. I daydream about sucking it straight from the straw until there's nothing left in it and the carton goes in on itself and makes a funny shape. But it's all we've got left now. And I have to share it with Mum anyway.

Suddenly, I have a really good idea and I wonder why I didn't think of it before: Michael's mum's flat. I bet she has things to drink in her kitchen. I didn't look around properly when I went in before but there will probably be something that we can drink. I'm sure of it.

Michael's mum's kitchen is really tidy and clean. There isn't a pile of dishes that are dirty on the side or anything like that. The cupboards have lots of things to eat inside them. Tins and packets and bottles of sauces, those kind of things. But there isn't much to drink.

I only find a bottle of orange squash on the side which is half empty. But you need to add water to squash to drink it and I don't know if you can drink it without water. I poke about in some other cupboards in the sitting room and there I find lots and lots of bottles of drink.

There are about ten bottles and they are all quite big. Some of them look like they have water in and others look like they are apple juice but when I look at them more closely, I see that they are bottles of drink which only adults have. Alcohol. But I'm not picky, it can't be that bad, and I carry them, and the bottle of squash, into our flat.

It takes a few trips. I open one that looks like water and pour it into a cup. It has a sharp smell. I take a sip but it tastes like poison and I can't swallow it. I spit it all out but I can still taste it and I hate it. I have to drink some orange squash without water to make it go away. It's a bit better but it coats my mouth with a sort of furriness that tastes sweet. I sniff some of the liquid that looks like apple juice but that smells even worse, so I don't even try it.

I curl up on the sofa and close my eyes. I'm going to fall asleep again but I'm so, so thirsty. More so than before. I can't stop thinking about lovely glasses of cool water, and then, before I know it, I'm dreaming about them. I dream I'm drinking water and then I dream that I'm in a bath and I can drink straight from the taps and the water in the bath even though it's full of bubbles. It's really cold in my mouth but I'm not feeling cold at all in the bath. I feel warm and happy. I'm just about to swim under the water when something jerks me awake.

It's a noise.

I wake so suddenly that I feel like I'm falling downwards but I'm not really, I'm just lying on the sofa.

The noise sounds like shuffling, like someone moving, but it isn't coming from Mum's room.

It's coming from outside our front door.

My heart is beating fast, like when you run around a lot and then stop and stand still. Your heart goes *bam, bam, bam* really quickly. You can hear it in your ears somehow.

I know I should go and see what it is but I don't want to. I sit as still as I can and wait to see if someone knocks on our door or says something. But there is just silence after that.

When I don't hear anything else, I go to our door and open it really, really slowly. I don't know what I expected to see but I never thought it would be what is sitting in front of me.

It is a huge bottle of water, sitting there like it has been waiting for me to open the door all this time.

There's no note on it or anything but I know it's for us. Someone has brought this to us. I look sideways down the corridor but there's no one there. The shuffling sounds I heard have long gone.

My first thought is that it is Gaia. I imagine her peering out at me from behind a pillar. I feel like I can see the shape of her hair poking out.

'Gaia!' I imagine saying.

And I picture her leaping out, her arms outstretched. 'Surprise, Ade! I bet you're thirsty by now.'

I keep looking down the corridor, willing Gaia to appear, but after staring for a while I realize there is no one there but me.

Chapter Twenty-eight

The bottle of water is so big that I have to use both arms to move it, and even then, I can only lift it a little way off the ground and I have to keep stopping. I half carry, half drag it into the kitchen.

I try to pour out a couple of glasses without spilling any. It's hard to do because it's so heavy and it's difficult for me to hold the bottle and the glass at the same time. I manage it in the end though, and then I'm drinking it.

I drink up my whole glass. I drink it so fast that I finish it after only a few seconds and I have to stop myself from drinking Mum's straight away afterwards too. I quickly take her glass in to her and then I come back and pour myself another. Nothing has ever tasted so good, which sounds silly because I never thought water tasted of anything before.

The label on the bottle has pictures of mountains on it. They are green but also have snow on the top. There's a blue sky and sunshine. I like the picture, so I tear it off to put in my book later. That's when I hear Mum get up.

'Where'd you get that from?' she's asking me.

'I found it outside,' I say. She goes to the kitchen and I hear her try to turn on the taps. It's a squeaky, dry sort of sound.

'Mum. The taps aren't working any more. Have some of this water.'

'Why aren't they working? We'd better get them fixed.' She yawns loudly and then drinks two whole glasses of water without stopping.

She doesn't know, I think. I thought that maybe she might have heard some of the news through the walls or looked out of the window, but she can't have. She doesn't know that everything has changed. I suddenly want to ask her if we'll be all right, but instead I tell her that.

'We'll be all right, Mum.'

'We will be, Ade.' And she kisses the top of my head. There's a moment as she walks back into her room when she pauses ever so slightly, like she's going to change direction and walk up to the window, to see what the world is doing. But

148

she carries on walking and closes the door of her bedroom behind her and I feel glad that she didn't look. It might be too big a shock to see the outside. There's not much left now.

I take another glass of water, luxuriating in its wetness as I swirl the liquid around my mouth. Then I start to ask myself who brought it to our door. Was it the rescue people who had come to get us? But why hadn't they knocked? Why did they only leave us water? I have to go and find them, whoever they were.

I leave the flat and walk up the stairs. The lifts aren't working, like everything else. I decide I'll walk past every flat from the top to the bottom to find who left us the water.

Everyone's door is closed like it always is, so in one way it's the same as any other day when I might go exploring in the tower. But the tower is missing all its sounds and smells and seems entirely different. Usually you'll hear kids shouting and mums shouting at them to be quiet, and you'll smell what's cooking for dinner or who's making a cake. I feel pretty sure that the flats I pass are all empty. There's no sounds or smells coming from them, just a stale kind of emptiness.

When I've gone down a few floors from my flat, I catch the smell of something which makes me stop.

It's a good smell, like meat cooking.

I press my ear against the door where I think it's coming from and listen. I can definitely hear someone inside moving things about but I don't knock. I just stand there and breathe in the smell. It's the most delicious smell, so good that just having it in my nostrils makes me feel like I'm eating it. Maybe it's chicken. Just like the chicken and rice Michael's mum made that night.

I'm thinking about food so much that I don't notice someone come up right behind me, so when he speaks to me, it makes me jump.

'Are you the kid from seventeen?'

I nod, thinking that this is the first person other than Mum that I've spoken to in days. I know him. He's the caretaker for the tower, who lives in the basement. He has a gruff sort of voice and he looks like he is a bit mad, but I know he is not from the next thing he does.

'You look like you could do with something to eat,' he says. And then he opens the door of the flat and leads me inside.

Chapter Twenty-nine

It isn't chicken but it's a little bit like it. The meat looks a bit darker but the skin is nice and crispy and it tastes just fine. I gobble up my plateful and drink down another good few cups of water. I'm so busy eating that only when I'm finished do I start to feel a bit uncomfortable that I'm sitting at a little red-and-white checked table with two people I've only just met.

Not many people ask you to come and sit down to eat with them when you don't know them at all. And Mum's always told me not to talk to strangers. But I guess this isn't like normal times any more, these are Blucher times and things are different.

There's Dory, whose flat we are sitting in. I've never met her before but she tells me that she has lived in the tower for a very long time. She has grey hair that looks like it might be quite long but it's all put up at the back of her head. She's wearing three cardigans. I notice them because they are all different colours. One's brown, one's dark red and one's a sort of yellow.

Dory wears a chain around her neck which has a large oval at the end of it. She sees me looking at it and she shows me that you can open it. There are pictures inside. They are little photographs of three people, and one of them is a baby, and she tells me that these are her children. I ask her if they live with her here but she shakes her head and doesn't say anything more for a little while.

And then there's Obi. I have seen him around a lot before, fixing things in the tower, but I never knew his name until today. He always looks like he's quite cross, even when we are sitting down to eat the food that Dory made. I've always had the feeling that he doesn't like kids much, but I think he must be the one who brought us the water. There is the same sort of bottle in Dory's flat. But Dory is far too small to be able to carry it. Under all her clothes, I don't think she can be much bigger than me.

I say to Obi, 'Thank you for the water.'

But he doesn't answer me back, he just sort of grunts as if to say, *That's nothing*.

'Is your mum OK, Ade?' Dory asks me.

'Yes,' I say, 'but she was getting thirsty before the water came.'

'Do you think she would like some lunch too?'

I don't know what to say then because I'm sure Mum would like some but I don't think she'd come down to Dory's flat to eat at the table like I have. So I say I'm not sure.

'I'll make her a plate up and then you can take it up to her. How about that?'

'That sounds great,' I say.

I like Dory. Her flat feels safe, and somehow it's not too quiet even with no television on. I think it's because it's full of interesting things.

There are lots and lots of books for one thing. Everywhere you look, there's another pile of them. Some of them are stacked so high they look like they might teeter over on top of you. There are books tucked into every little bit of space you can think of: under the armchair, on top of the kitchen cupboards. I've never seen so many in my whole life.

I like the books. We haven't got very many in

our house. I have a handful in my bedroom but they're scrappy and some of them are torn. These books look golden somehow. The pages have yellowed with age, just like Dory herself has wrinkled. They're old friends to her.

And then, among the books, there are all kinds of bits and pieces. Odd seashells, old typewriters, a giant empty white birdcage. There's a little bowl which has strips of white paper inside.

'Pick a fortune,' Dory says. I take one out and it reads:

Your present question marks are going to succeed.

'You keep it,' says Dory, and I put it carefully into my pocket. I'll stick it into my book later.

'Here, Ade. For your mum. You'll tell her we say hi, won't you?'

Dory gives me a plate of steaming food. It smells good. I thank her and I get up to go.

Obi opens the door for me. I can't do it because I'm holding the plate.

I stop for a moment.

I want to come back to Dory's flat later but I don't know how to ask. I want to see them again soon and not feel lonely in the flat any more while Mum is sleeping.

It's as if they are reading my mind because Dory says, 'Come back any time and I certainly want to see you for dinner, young man.'

And then Obi says, 'I'll bring you some more water later.'

And as I carefully walk up the stairs trying not to spill any of Mum's lunch, I feel happier than I have in a long time.

Chapter Thirty

'We'll put this one up here and one in the bathroom and here's your torch.'

Obi gives me a pink torch and shows me how to pull out the handle and wind it up. He's brought us a couple of lanterns for our flat and a torch each for me and Mum.

He doesn't ask to see Mum but gives me her torch to give to her. It's yellow.

'You show your mum how to wind it up, OK, kid?' he says.

I know he's going to go soon. He's just walked up with me to bring the lantern and torches after we had dinner with Dory. I had to carry Mum's plate again.

We had a pie tonight and Dory put this funny little china blackbird in the middle of it, so you could just see its head and beak poking out of the top of the pie.

She said, 'We have Obi to thank for the pastry.'

I didn't know what she meant so I said to him, 'Did you make it?'

He gave a small chuckle then and said, 'No, Dory just means I found the ingredients.'

'Right, I'll be off now. See you in the morning, kid.'

I say, 'Good night, Obi, and thanks for the torches.'

And he's gone.

Mum's sleeping, with her back turned towards me. It's hard to do it without making any noise but I try to put Mum's plate on her bedside table as quietly as I can and take away the one I brought up at lunchtime that's empty now. I wish she was awake so I could tell her about Obi and Dory. I want to tell her that I'm all right, that there's someone looking after me. It feels important that she knows. But I don't wake her. I leave her a torch and tiptoe out. I'll have to show her how to wind it up later.

They're really good torches because they'll never run out of batteries. You just have to turn the handle a few times and the light comes on. I decide to wind mine up lots and lots, so it won't run out for a really long time.

I take a bit of time drawing Dory and Obi into my scrapbook. I think I get Dory right but I find Obi hard to draw. It's difficult to draw someone who is cross and kind at the same time.

Then I switch the lantern off and play with my torch, lying on the sofa. I don't mind the dark as much now that I have it. I make the beam move all over the room, so I can see every little part of it. I see things that I wouldn't normally see if the lights were on. I see a little crack in the ceiling that goes all the way from one wall to the other, and I find a thin, floaty spider's web that hangs in one corner of the room. I make shadow animals out of my hands and they dance on the ceiling and march to the window.

And that's when I see it. Another light.

A torch from the block opposite mine.

From Gaia's block.

I flash my torch on and off, on and off from my window and I wait.

The torch in Gaia's block blinks on and off, on and off back at me.

The next time I switch it off quickly three times, so it flashes, and then leave it on for a moment at the end before I turn it off. I look out at the tower and see the same pattern being repeated back.

I have heard of a code that people use with torches going on and off again, but I don't know it and I get the feeling the other person doesn't either. We just keep copying each other's torch light patterns over and over. We are not able to make words but I think what we are saying to each other is more important than that. We are saying, *I'm here, you're here and I can see you.*

Our torch signalling goes on into the night until the other person leaves their beam on and waves it from side to side and then switches it off.

I think they are waving goodbye. Saying good night.

I try to sleep but I can't stop thinking about the light I just saw from the other block. It looked like it could have come from the same floor as me. The seventeenth floor. It didn't seem to be any higher or lower than my flat.

I can't help but wonder if it was Gaia who was signalling to me.

And what if she wasn't signalling me just to tell me she was there? What if she was trying to tell me that she needed help?

Chapter Thirty-one

The next morning when I wake up, the very first thing I do is look out of the window at Gaia's tower.

From where I am I can see that the Bluchers have completely surrounded the block. Even from so high up, I can see their glistening blue bodies entangled with one another, and, terrifyingly, I see that they are moving. Are they swaying in the wind or raging towards Gaia's tower, reaching forward to their next meal? The ground all around the tower is thick with them. A mass of blue.

And I can see, with deadly certainty, that they have started to feed. It is the same with all the other blocks that are still standing. I can almost sense the Bluchers' hunger in the way they have gathered around the bottom of each building, their silvery-blue colour pulsing as they push forward. Like how sometimes you can see your heartbeat on your wrist. It's not a big movement but it doesn't stop. One pulse follows another and then another and then another. And it won't stop until that building has gone.

Whatever it is they are doing, it won't be too long before they eat away so much at the bottom that the blocks will all just collapse. I can see that the lower parts of the buildings are already a little thinner. They won't last long.

I count up seventeen windows to find Gaia's flat. I try to look really hard to see if anyone is moving inside but it's too far away. But I know there is someone there and that if I don't do something, I will watch the tower fall knowing that there is a person trapped inside. And the part that I don't want to say out loud to myself is that the person might be Gaia.

I have to find Obi.

He will know what to do.

I run downstairs to find him. I stop at Dory's flat first because I think she might know where Obi is.

Dory opens the door straight away and says, 'Good timing, Ade, I've just put some porridge on,' but she stops talking when she sees my face.

Dory sends me downstairs to the basement to find Obi. She doesn't ask me what's wrong or tell me to calm down, she just looks at my face and says, 'Try the basement, Ade.'

I hardly ever come down here. There are big thick pipes that run along the ceiling and only very small rectangular windows, so without the lights on, it's hard to see where you are walking. Part of me feels afraid, an old fear that you could get lost in these corridors and never get out, as if it was a maze or a labyrinth rather than just a bunch of rooms and hallways. I put the thought out of my mind and start walking, shouting out Obi's name as I go.

'You scared me, kid,' Obi says when he pokes his head out of a doorway.

That's a joke, I think. *How could I scare anyone?*

I tell Obi about the torch signals, how I think it might be my friend Gaia and how the Bluchers have surrounded the other buildings.

Obi doesn't say anything as I speak. He frowns and rubs his face quite a lot but he doesn't speak until I've finished.

I've been so worried about Gaia and so glad to see Obi that I've barely noticed the room we are in. You know when you are feeling and thinking about two things at exactly the same time and they take up all the space in your brain? When I finish talking, I look around me and take in where we are.

I guess I must be in Obi's flat but it's tiny, just one room, really, and quite a small one at that. There's a single bed that has a red and green blanket on it, neatly tucked in, and a little chest of drawers, but not much else.

It almost looks like it could belong to anyone, but there are lots and lots of framed photographs on Obi's chest of drawers. I can see Obi in one of them standing next to a lady, but he's smiling from ear to ear, so it might not be him. Perhaps it's his identical twin.

I open my mouth to ask him who it is but then I remember, in a rushing flood, why I came to find Obi. I think of Gaia, trapped in the tower, the blue swarm of Bluchers hungrily feasting at the foundations of her building.

'Please help,' I say instead.

When Obi talks, it's so slow and quiet that I have to strain my ears to hear him.

'We must try to rescue them,' he says.

'But what about the spores?'

'We must try,' he says again.

Chapter Thirty-two

Over the next hour, I learn more and more about Obi's job as a caretaker. I find out that he has a bunch of keys that can open every door in the tower. Imagine: he could go into anyone's flat at any time.

'Only if I need to fix things, Ade,' Obi tells me as I stare open-mouthed at the set of shiny brass keys. 'Not just because I fancy it.'

'But you can open *any* door in this building?'

'Yes, of course.'

'Even the door to my flat?'

'Yes.'

'Have you ever had to do that?' I ask, looking at Obi out of the corner of my eye.

'Your mum's let me in in the past, so I haven't had to.'

'Oh,' I said.

'How is your mum doing?' Obi says, quietly and quickly.

'She's all right,' I say. 'She . . . she . . .'

'It's OK, Ade. As long as she's all right.'

'I don't think she knows what's going on,' I continue.

'Ah,' says Obi. 'That must be difficult.'

'Well,' I say, not wanting to say yes or no.

'It's hard not to talk through things with someone you love.'

'Who do you talk to?' I ask.

Obi chuckles a bit, although I don't know why. 'Me?' He scratches his beard thoughtfully. 'Well, I guess I talk to Dory.'

'Do you love Dory, then?'

'Well, Dory's a splendid woman. Maybe I do love her in some ways, but . . .' Obi goes quiet then and I start thinking about the woman in the photo. I wonder if that's the person Obi loves.

'But?' I say.

'Well, things change, don't they?'

'Is this the woman you love?' I ask, and I point to the framed photograph sitting on the chest of drawers.

Obi picks it up and stares at it thoughtfully.

'Cicely,' he says. 'Cicely was a wonderful woman.'

'Where is she now?'

Obi looks at me sharply and puts the frame back onto the chest so violently that it falls over on its face. He has to pick it up and stand it back up again properly.

'She left,' he says simply. He stands up. The conversation is over.

'Now, let's go and help your Gaia. Before those Bluchers get any further.'

Obi walks out of the tiny room and I spend a moment more looking at those smiling faces. Cicely's bright, friendly smile. And I know now who the other person is. It isn't Obi's twin. It's Obi, when he was very happy.

I run to catch up with Obi, who's already disappearing down the corridor.

I soon learn that Obi knows about everyone living in the tower. He doesn't just know about my mum. He knows about Michael's mum and that she's good at cooking. He knows about the man on the second floor who never used to leave his flat. He wasn't like Mum, though; it was because he was too old. He had someone come round to bring him meals every day and when the buildings started falling, his daughter came and took him away.

He knows about the family with the mum who always made nice cakes. He knows about the woman who owned a cat that had kittens. He knows about everyone.

He takes me to a flat on one of the lower floors.

It has a funny, medicine smell about it. A bit like the stuff that people pour onto a cut and they say it won't hurt, but it does. Everything in the flat is brown, the chairs, the sofa, even the walls and the lampshades.

Obi picks up two tall silver bottles which have thin clear plastic wires with a mask attached to them from behind one of the chairs. Then we go to a flat a few floors up.

It's full of large photographs of jungles and deserts and things like that. There's a large vase of flowers that have died on a table in the sitting room, and lots and lots of books too. But unlike Dory's books, which look like they've been read about ten times, these ones are shiny and big, glossy and new-looking.

Obi comes out of the bedroom with one of those really big rucksacks that look so huge you can't imagine how one person can carry it on their back. He gives it to me to carry. Although it's so big, with nothing in it, it's quite light. Then we go back down to Obi's room in the basement, Obi carrying the oxygen tanks and me, the rucksack.

Obi hands me a roll of white tape. 'You've got to stick this over the mask, kid, when I tell you. No holes, OK?'

He has put the silver bottles into the bag and fiddled with the top of one of the bottle, so we hear a little hissing sound. Then he puts the rucksack on his back and sits on the bed. He puts the mask on and tells me to cover it.

I try my best, I really do, but I'm worried. The woman on the TV said the spores are tiny and I'm sure they could get through the tape. When I'm done, Obi takes a scarf out of his drawer and wraps that over his face as well, so you can just about see his eyes but that is all. Then he pulls out a pair of swimming goggles and puts those on too.

He looks mad but he says, 'You can't be too careful,' and I agree.

'Wait in Dory's flat for me. Don't come down-stairs, whatever you do. Promise me, Ade. I might let spores into the tower when I go out, so you must wait with Dory.'

'OK,' I say. 'Good luck.'

But it doesn't seem enough to just say that.

Because what I'm thinking is, *Please, please be all right, please, please come back, please, please save Gaia.*

And I'm thinking that Obi is the bravest man I have ever met.

Chapter Thirty-three

It's been about two hours since Obi left the tower.

Dory went white when I told her where he'd gone but she sort of shook her head quickly and said, 'He'll be back soon,' and now she's teaching me how to play Gin Rummy.

I haven't played cards before, properly. I like the ones with the faces that are called the jack and the king and the queen. I tell Dory that and she says, 'Why don't we give them all faces?' So we do just that. We both draw silly little eyes and smiles on each one. Dory's good at drawing. She even makes one of them look a bit like me. Even I can see it's got my fuzzy hair and my little smile that doesn't look like it's fully finished. It's the two of diamonds.

Gin Rummy is fun. It's miles better than any of the games I play by myself. Even the animal game. It goes on for quite a long time, too.

Dory tells me the rules. She gives us each seven cards and says that I need to collect three of one thing and four of another. Either the same number card, so three jacks or four sevens, or what Dory calls a run. That's when you have the numbers going up like three, four, five. It's hard to get a run though, because they have to all be in the same suit, clubs or hearts or whatever.

I thought I'd won ages ago and shouted out, 'Rummy!' like Dory told me to, but my run wasn't in the same suit, so we had to keep going.

I'm collecting cards with the same number now. It's easier. I just need one more card, the five of spades, and I've won.

We don't talk as we play but Dory grins at me from over the top of her cards a lot. I think she's enjoying playing.

'Rummy!' Dory shouts and she slaps her cards on the table so hard that it shakes.

We play a few more times. Dory wins twice and I win once. Then it's lunchtime.

'Do you want to go see your mum while I get lunch together, Ade?' she asks me.

'Can I just wait with you until Obi comes back?' I say.

'Of course,' says Dory. 'You can give me a hand with lunch.'

She asks me if I know how to chop an onion and when I say I think so, she gives me a couple that have sprouted green shoots from the top and a little knife and a chopping board.

I'm not very good at it, as it turns out, so Dory shows me what to do. You make a sort of a bridge with one hand to hold the onion steady and then you cut it in half. Then you take off the top bit that's got the green coming out of it and peel off the brown, papery skin. And only after you've done all that can you start chopping.

'We need the pieces to be quite small,' Dory says, so it takes quite a while to slice them into little bits.

My eyes begin to sting, and even though I don't mean to, I find that I'm crying. Tears are running down my face and dripping over the onions.

'Why am I crying, Dory?' I ask. 'Is it the onions or is it about Obi?'

Or is it about Gaia? I think to myself.

'It's the onions, Ade. They make everyone cry. I like them for it. It's good to have a good cry sometimes.'

I'm not sure I agree. I have to keep stopping and wiping my eyes because the tears blur my vision and I can't see what I'm doing. But finally I finish chopping and Dory fries them up over a little flame that comes out of a small blue canister. Dory says that people use them for camping and that Obi had found quite a few in the tower.

The large copper pan is so much bigger than the little cooker, it looks like it might fall off, but Dory keeps one hand wrapped in a tea towel around the handle.

She asks me to hold it while she rummages around in a box on the floor for a couple of tins. One's corned beef and the other's chopped tomatoes. She adds both of them to the pan with the onions and soon her flat is filled with a rich cooking smell. Then she adds in a packet of ready-cooked white rice, and after that she spoons it into four bowls. One for me, one for her, one for Mum and one for Obi.

'Eat up,' Dory says. We sit at the table, not talking for a bit, finishing up the food.

'I'd better take Mum's upstairs,' I say, and Dory opens the door for me even though I can carry the bowl OK with one hand.

As soon as I open the door to my flat, I know something's wrong. I can hear the sound of something breaking, a smashing, splintering sound that makes me think of someone screaming.

'Mum?' I call out.

As if in answer, I hear another crash.

'Mum!' I'm worried now. Something's not right.

I go into the sitting room and place Mum's lunch on the table. She's not in there. I hear another smash coming from the kitchen and that's where I find her. She has a plate in her hand that she's about to drop to the floor, and as she releases it, I dash forward and surprise myself by catching it in mid air. I place it gingerly on the side but Mum tries to pick it up again.

'Stop it, Mum!' I cry. She looks at me and it seems to take her a moment to register who I am, and to remind her, I say, 'It's me, Mum. Ade.'

She starts to cry then. Glassy tears that look too large to be real spring from her eyes.

'What's happened to us?' she says. 'What's happened?'

She makes a howling sound or a moan, I'm not sure which, and the tears keep pouring from her eyes.

'It's OK, Mum,' I say, and I lead her over the smashed plates and then see that she's not wearing shoes and I worry that she's going to cut her feet but I need to get her out of our grey little kitchen and away from the rest of the plates.

Mum runs to the window when we're in the sitting room and bangs her wrists against the glass, so the panes rattle and shake.

'What's happened? What's happened?'

'It's the Bluchers, Mum,' I say, but of course that doesn't help because Mum doesn't know what they are.

'Why? Why?' she cries, and she tucks herself up into a small, tight ball in front of the window.

'It's OK, Mum. We're going to be OK.' I stroke her back, which is shaking from her cries. 'It's OK.' I say it over and over until even I start to believe it.

'Why don't you go back to bed now, Mum?' I say, and I didn't think Mum was listening to me really but she starts to stand as soon as I suggest it and we slowly walk together towards her room, Mum leaning on me as if I was a walking stick.

She climbs into bed by herself and I leave her lunch on the side table. I watch her for a few minutes before I turn away, closing the door quietly behind me.

There is silence in the flat once more. I go to the kitchen and try to clear up the smashed plates as well as I can but I keep finding more and more little fragments that I've missed. They are thin and sharp and one of them sticks into my finger, making me wince and cry out.

I miss Dory's company and I want to go back there but I can't help looking out of the window at Gaia's tower. I wonder if I'll be able to see Obi out there. For one dreadful moment, I look down and my eyes search the ground to see if there is someone lying there, and I let myself breathe again when I can't see anyone.

Obi must have made it inside, but why has he not returned yet?

Already I can see the damage that the Bluchers are doing to the tower. It looks like it has shed another layer of skin. It won't be able to stay standing for much longer.

The next thing I think is so simple that I can't believe it's taken me so long to work it out.

Before I met Obi and Dory, I'd been worried that our tower was going to fall, that the Bluchers would start eating it as well. Meeting them has made me feel safer. Like I haven't had to look behind me all the time. But how can they stop our tower from falling? How can anyone be protected from the Bluchers? Surely we are also in danger?

I wonder if the people in the other tower can see that our building is being eaten away, just like I can see that theirs is? And even if Obi manages to find them, why would they leave one falling-down home for another?

But at the same time I think this, I know it can't be true. I've been down to the basement today and there isn't any damage. There aren't any holes or cracks in the lower walls. I know because I walked right past them.

But why not?

I sit up on the sill and put my head right next to the window, so I can look directly down. There is a thick cluster of silvery Bluchers surrounding us, but for some reason they are not touching our walls.

It is as if there is a protective force field that they can't get past. A little gap of space between them and us which means they can't eat away at our walls.

Something is stopping the Bluchers in their tracks.

Chapter Thirty-four

There is nothing to do but wait for Obi to get back.

I go back to Dory's flat and she calls me in. I find her sitting on one of her orange armchairs with her feet propped up on a little table, reading a book.

'Do you like reading?' she asks me.

'I guess so,' I say. She says, she has some books I might like the look of and starts picking up piles here and there to find them.

'Try these,' she says, and hands me a few.

I pick one that just has a single word as its title: *Boy*.

It's about someone growing up and the funny things they remember from when they are a child.

It takes me a little while to get into it, but soon I am right there next to him. He's jumping into the sea on holiday in Norway. And now he's putting a dead mouse into a jar of gobstoppers in a sweetshop.

It seems like a faraway land to me, full of exciting things happening. And it fills my head with colour too. The blue of the sea, the craggy green islands, the orange spotty fish that he eats. It's quite unlike the grey buildings and roads that used to surround us, and the weird sort of silver of the Bluchers now. I like it. It makes me forget for a minute or two that we are still waiting for Obi to come back.

Just as I am reading about the island, we hear footsteps coming down the corridor.

Dory and I look at each other for a quick moment, and then we both spring up and rush to the front door. Obi is standing there frowning, as if he is surprised to see us.

I throw my arms around him, I am so glad to see him. He gives me a little pat on the back. I don't think he knows what else to do.

'Did you find anyone?' Dory asks. 'Did you bring anyone back?'

Obi sits down heavily on one of the chairs.

'Yes,' he says.

We both wait for him to say more but he

doesn't. There is a big silence that I know I shouldn't break, but I have to.

'Did you find Gaia?' I ask in a small voice.

Obi looks at me then.

'No. There were no kids there.'

Then he looks away and none of us say anything.

We sit there for quite a while like that.

I have to stop myself from asking all the questions that are rising up in me like bubbles that are going to pop: *Did you go to Gaia's flat? Did it look like they had left? Had she left me a note or anything?*

Instead I just have to wonder: *Who it is that Obi has brought to live with us?*

Chapter Thirty-five

Only when Dory starts making dinner does she ask Obi again about who he found in Gaia's tower.

'Will they be eating, Obi? I need to know how much to make.'

He just says, 'Make one more plate up.'

So that's how we first know it's just one other person.

I really want to ask who it is and why they haven't come to Dory's flat to say hello and do they know where Gaia is, but Obi looks tired, like there's something else that he's thinking about all the time, so I just help Dory with dinner and don't say anything.

It's pasta with walnuts tonight. I've never had it before and I want to say that I don't like nuts really but I don't feel I can.

Obi disappears with a plate of food after

dinner and Dory asks me if I want to play Gin Rummy again before bed. We play twice, one win each, and then I go back upstairs to Mum.

It's strange that Obi won't tell us what happened. I ask Dory if she knows why but she just says, 'He must have his reasons,' and, 'We mustn't rush him.'

It's a funny kind of sleep that night. There are no torch signals from the other tower any more. Just complete blackness outside. Even though I know there's not just Mum now, but Obi and Dory too, I feel lonely somehow.

There's a moment in the middle of the night when I'm woken by the most terrific crashing sound.

It sounds like a groan and a bang and a smash all at the same time.

It terrifies me, it's so loud and close. My windows rattle and shake as if they've been hit with something. Something hard.

Then I realize I know what it is.

Gaia's tower has finally fallen.

Chapter Thirty-six

The next morning I ask Obi and Dory if I can do something to help. They're talking about how much food we have left and how long it will last us.

I haven't been listening properly to what they've been saying.

And then Obi says, 'Ade, you can help with that, OK?'

'Yes, you'll do a fine job,' says Dory.

I look up at their smiling, nodding faces and they tell me what they want me to do.

My job is to go into flats and bring back any food we can eat.

I also need to tell Obi if I find any water.

Since Gaia's tower fell, I haven't felt much like doing anything. Obi said that she wasn't there but I know he didn't have time to look everywhere in the block. What if she was hiding somewhere; somewhere other than her flat?

I really want to ask Obi more about it but I don't like to ask him lots of questions. It's not that I'm scared of him or anything, I'm just not sure he would like it.

It's good to be doing something other than sitting around but it doesn't stop me from thinking about Gaia. I can't stop remembering times when we were together. Everything reminds me of her.

Eating dinner with Obi and Dory reminds me of the time just after I'd told Gaia about Mum not leaving the flat. She asked me if I would like to come round for dinner at her flat.

'Come tonight,' she said. 'We'll go straight to mine.'

'Does your mum know? Have you asked her?'

'No,' said Gaia, looking surprised that I'd asked. 'She'd say no if I asked her, but if you just turn up, she won't be able to.'

'I don't know,' I said. There was some sort of unwritten rule that Gaia and I could only see each other at school. I'm not sure how it came about exactly but sometimes adults don't need to tell us what to do all the time; we can sense what they want.

'Your mum never has to know!' exclaimed Gaia. 'And you can see my garden. The mint is really tasty in tea. C'mon, Ade! Jollof! Tell me you don't want it!'

I knew how kind Gaia was being. She was willing to risk her mum being annoyed with her to make sure I had a proper dinner, but I couldn't bring myself to say yes. It felt like I would have crossed over a line if I had gone, not saying anything to Mum when I got back, while my belly was full from Gaia's mum's cooking.

'Fine. Suit yourself,' Gaia said, and I could tell she was cross with me.

'It's just . . . Mum . . .'

'It's fine, Ade. I said it was fine.'

Sometimes it's those memories that are the most painful of all. More so than the happy ones. I hope that one day I may get the chance to say sorry to her.

I decide to ask the person that Obi brought back if they know what happened to her family, as soon as I can. Until then, I just think in my head: *You're all right, Gaia, you're all right, Gaia, you're all right, Gaia,* because everyone knows if you think about something enough then there's a good chance it'll come true.

We've decided to put all the food into one of the flats next to Dory's, so we can see how much we have. There isn't space to store it all at Dory's. Obi gives me one of those bags with wheels at the bottom that you pull behind you, to carry the food in. He tells me to start from the top floor and gives me a large bunch of keys so I can open everyone's door.

I have to leave them unlocked because we need to start using everyone else's toilets now. Ours aren't flushing any more, so we have to start using different ones or the smell will get too bad.

The first flat I go into has lots and lots of food in it. It looks like a big family lived here. There are lots of kids' drawings stuck onto the fridge and toys scattered about the sitting room. I think they must have left in a hurry because there are heaps of clothes about the place and drawers left open. I don't look around the flat much, though, I just head to the kitchen.

Even though everyone has gone, it's strange to go into these people's homes. It was a bit different when I went into Michael's mum's flat because I knew them and I had been there before. This feels a bit different, like I'm trespassing. But we need to eat and the people who lived here don't need the food right now, so I pull a chair over to be able to open the cupboards. They are full of things we can take. And that's when I have a good idea. I'll do the same as I did when I took the tins of beans and bag of rice from Michael's mum's flat: I'll keep a list of everything I take from every flat I go into. If the tower stays standing and the world goes back to normal and the people who live here come back, then we'll just replace everything that we took using my list.

It makes me feel a lot better about taking the food. I run off to my flat and find my scrapbook and a pen so I can start straight away. I write the flat number at the top of the page and then I start my list. There's cans of coconut milk and bags of rice and brown beans. I find some old yams which will still be OK to eat, but not any other kind of vegetable. Obi told me not to open the fridges. They've been off for a long time now, so everything will be bad inside them.

I fill the bag quickly and there's still plenty to come back for. And then I start the trip downstairs to Dory's floor. It takes quite a long time because of all the stairs and the bag is heavy. It judders down each step with a loud thump.

Finally I reach the flat we're keeping the food in and Dory is there waiting.

She takes everything out and starts sorting through what I've found. Her job is to put everything away. I go back upstairs with my empty bag, but on the way I stop at my flat and go to my bedroom to find my red rucksack. It's not as big as the one Obi gave me but it's big enough, and much easier to carry.

The next time I just fill my rucksack, and that means I can run down the stairs with the food. I can't carry as much each time but it makes me much faster, and after a few runs up and down the food is starting to pile up. There are lots of tins and bags of food and bottles of oil. I also find quite a few packets of biscuits, and in one flat, six bars of chocolate.

'I think it's time for a rest. And lunch,' Dory says.

She picks up a couple of tins from a large stack and we go back into her flat. It's potato and leek soup. I've never had it before and I'm not sure if I'll like it.

Dory sees my spoon hovering over the bowl.

'Even if you don't like it, Ade, you must eat some,' she says.

It doesn't taste too bad. In fact, it doesn't taste much of anything. When we've finished eating, we play a quick game of cards before we get back to work.

Obi doesn't come to eat with us today. Dory says we'll see him later. Before I leave, Dory gives me a box of crackers to take Mum with a little bowl of the soup.

The day seems to be over more quickly than usual. I find some good things after lunch. Some big bottles of water that I'll tell Obi about later, and a large orange net bag of onions which Dory was really pleased about. My scrapbook's filling up with all the lists of food. I must have done about four pages today.

Before I know it, I can hear Dory and Obi's voices from inside Dory's flat and I can smell something cooking for dinner. When I get to the front door, though, I don't go in straight away. I'm not sure why.

I wait for a moment and listen to what they are saying.

It's about how upset someone is.

They must be talking about the person Obi rescued from the other tower. I hear Obi say, 'He's not in a good way,' and, 'No one should have to see that,' and, 'We'll have to keep an eye on him.' And then they start talking about the food we have and I go in.

After dinner, Dory says that I've worked hard today so I should go to the flat where we're storing all the food and pick something for dessert.

It's a little bit like being in a funny sort of shop. I go to the sofa where Dory said she put all the sweet things and there's a big pile of different types of biscuits, bags of cakes that look like little boats and large blocks of chocolate.

I have to rummage around for a little while before I find what I'm looking for. I found it in the first flat I went into this morning. A little plastic box full of chin chin. Little crunchy pieces of chin chin.

Mum used to make it for me as a treat but I haven't had it in a long time. She used to let me cut the dough into small squares and then she would drop them into a pan of hot oil to fry them. She'd stir, stir, stir and then scoop them out of the pan onto a plate with a square of kitchen roll on it. The smell they'd make when they were cooking used to hang around for days afterwards, long after we had finished eating them all.

I shake the little box that I found and it rattles.

'Good choice, kid,' Obi says, and we sit eating the chin chin until it's all gone.

Chapter Thirty-seven

The next day is much the same. I bring food from the top floor down to Dory and she puts it all into different piles in the flat. All the bags of rice and pasta are kept in the bath, bottles are put in the kitchen and tins are kept in the bedroom.

Dory says I can take a break from carrying the food after lunch and tells me to arrange the tins for a bit. I spend a long time building them up into a castle with four tall turrets at each corner and battlements at the top of the walls. Dory laughs when she sees it.

'That wasn't exactly what I meant, Ade, but a splendid piece of work, nonetheless,' she says, and I feel pinkly glad from her praise.

Sometimes it feels like it has always been Dory, Obi and me and that it will go on this way, unchanging, for ever. That evening, though, as I approach Dory's door for dinner, I hear something new, something different. It isn't Obi's low, deep rumble of a voice or Dory's singsong way of speaking; it is someone else, someone new. I stop myself from opening the door straight away as though I want to prepare myself.

It must be the person from Gaia's tower, the person that Obi rescued. Someone who might be able to tell me where Gaia is. They might know her. They might have seen her leave, perhaps. My heart seems to skip two beats, one after another, and I feel excited and oddly nervous, which makes me dally in the doorway for just a few more minutes before I knock on the door.

'That's Ade,' I hear Dory say. 'Come in, Ade!'

I push the door open slowly.

'Now, Ade, what have I told you about knocking?' Dory chides. 'You know you can come straight in.'

There is a tall thin man sitting at the table. He has sandy hair that looks like it is a bit overgrown and a wiry blond beard that makes his face look quite long.

Dory says to me, 'This is Ben, Ade, say hello.'

'Hello, Ben,' I say. I pause. I want to ask him

about Gaia straight away but something about the way he looks stops me.

Ben's eyes are red as if he has rubbed them really, really hard and his hair is sticking up all over the place and looks greasy.

Of course, we are all looking a bit grubby these days. We don't wash hardly at all any more. Water is too precious to waste on washing, Obi says. Instead, we've all got lots of packs of baby wipes which we use but there's nothing we can do about our hair. I've never seen Obi's hair sticking up like that, though.

I decide to wait until later to ask Ben if he knows Gaia and if she left the tower.

Ben doesn't talk much that evening. He doesn't join in when Dory, Obi and I tell each other what our favourite animals are. (Me: dog, Dory: elephant, Obi: gorilla.) And he doesn't say, 'That's great, Dory, thanks for dinner,' when he finishes eating, like Obi and I always do.

He just sits there, eating really slowly. After I finish, Dory spoons out some food on a plate for me to take up to Mum.

'Do you want to take this now, Ade, and then come back for some cards? Or shall we see you in the morning?'

I'm just about to say, 'I'll come back,' when Ben starts speaking.

'Where's his mum?' he says.

And he looks from me to Dory to Obi.

No one says anything.

It's one of the things that from the very beginning made me like Dory and Obi. They've always seemed to know, without me telling them, that I don't want to talk about Mum not coming out of our flat. It's not that we don't talk about Mum. They often say, 'How's your mum doing, Ade?' or, 'I hope your mum likes dinner tonight.' And sometimes I tell them little stories about Mum and me. But they've never asked me, 'Why don't we see your mum?' or, 'What's wrong with your mum, Ade?' And they never sound angry or cross with her when we do talk about her.

Not like Michael's mum. She used to say to me all the time, 'I don't know what that mother of yours is thinking.' She would sound so mad when she said it, it was as if she was spitting the words from her mouth, like orange pips.

'Why isn't she with him?' Ben is saying now. His voice is getting louder now and his stare is getting harder as he looks at each one of us. I think I can feel it zapping me in the face through the air.

I can see that Dory and Obi are trying to think of the right thing to say. They don't want to tell him that Mum can't leave the flat, but at the same time there isn't much more to say than that. So I just tell him.

'Oh,' says Ben. 'Can't she walk very well?'

'No, it's not like that,' I say. 'She doesn't want to go out of the flat. She doesn't like it so much that she can't do it.'

Ben is looking at me so hard now that his eyes start watering. Then I realize his eyes aren't watering, he's crying. Dory puts a hand on his shoulder because he's really sobbing now and he's not looking at me any more, he's put his face right down onto his plate of food.

'Come on, Ade,' Obi says, 'I'll walk up with you.'

I stand up, and even though I don't want to go because I haven't asked Ben about Gaia yet, I walk to the door with Obi. We leave Dory's flat and start climbing up the stairs. Because it's summer there's still plenty of daylight until quite late, which means we don't need to worry about taking torches around with us after dinner. I say this to Obi and he nods.

'Why did Ben cry when I told him about Mum?' I ask.

And what Obi tells me next really surprises me because I thought Mum was the only person who didn't like going out.

'Ben had a wife who was a bit like your mum,' he says. 'She didn't like leaving her bedroom. But she died. And that's why he's so sad.'

I can't believe that there are other people like Mum. Especially that there was someone like Mum who didn't live very far away, who was only down the street in Gaia's tower.

I suppose that only the people who really couldn't leave would have stayed, like Mum and then me because I won't leave her, and Ben's wife and then Ben because he wouldn't leave her.

I wonder why Dory and Obi stayed. I'll ask them sometime. They must have a reason too.

I suppose there are so many of us in all these towers, all on top of each other, one family above another and another and another so that we are stretching to the sky, that maybe it's not so strange that there was someone like Mum in Gaia's tower.

Maybe there was another Dory and another Obi too.

Perhaps there was another Ade.

And then we're at my flat. Obi tells me to

wait for a little while but to come back down in a bit if I want to. Then he leaves and I listen to his footsteps disappear down the corridor.

Mum's bedroom is quiet and dark. I pull open the curtain a crack, so the last of the day's sunlight makes a yellow line on the wall.

Mum doesn't wake up. I take her dirty plate and carefully place her dinner on the table. It's funny to think she hasn't met Obi or Dory or even Ben. I wonder if she wants to know how I'm getting all this food now and where I go all day. Does she think I'm still going to school? Has she looked outside and seen what the Bluchers have done?

I look at her sleeping face.

She is so still and silent but I can hear the tiny sighs as she breathes in and out. I leave her then, tiptoe out of the room and close the door behind me.

Only when I'm walking back down to Dory's flat do I remember that I forgot to shut the curtain, but the thought makes me feel glad somehow. Because I know that tomorrow morning, Mum will wake up in the sunshine.

Not in darkness.

Chapter Thirty-eight

The next night Dory asks me to take a plate of dinner to Ben. I suppose he doesn't want to eat with us for some reason. He has moved into a flat on the floor below Dory.

Dinner was what Dory called a 'mish-mash' tonight. Some rice, some kidney beans, little chopped-up onions and thick slices of frankfurter sausage, all fried up together. I liked it.

I knock on his door and Ben calls me in. He is lying on the sofa, looking straight up at the ceiling. He doesn't move when I come in. I put the plate down on a little table and go into his kitchen to find a fork for him.

I put the fork down carefully next to the plate and say, 'It's nice and tasty.'

Ben says, 'Dory's good at cooking,' which surprises me because I don't think he has ever said that to her.

I think of asking about Gaia, but Ben's looking away from me like he wants me to go, so I walk to the door to leave. Then I hear him call out to me. 'Ade, come back here a moment.'

I walk back into the room and see that Ben is sitting up now, looking directly ahead.

'How's your mum doing? Is she coping OK?'

'I think so,' I say.

'When my wife Evie found out about the spores, I thought she was glad that there was a real reason why she couldn't go outside. I couldn't force her any more because she would say, "But what about the spores? We can't leave the block now."'

He pauses and then asks, 'Does your mum do that?'

I don't say anything but I come to sit down next to Ben.

We both sit looking forward, not looking at each other. Ben keeps talking.

'I pleaded with Evie to leave. You know, when everyone was packing up. I told her that our tower would fall if we stayed there, that we would die when that happened, but it didn't bother her. She didn't hear what I was saying. She'd stopped hearing me. I knew she couldn't do it, she hadn't been outside for five years, but I couldn't stop pleading with her, trying to reason with her.

'Then one morning we woke up and it was so quiet. I thought we were the only ones left here. Everything stopped working, the water, the electricity, and I knew we didn't have long. The Bluchers were taking control and there was no one to stop them.

'And then there was the night I saw the lights coming from this tower. It was you, right? Obi said it was you . . .'

I nod.

'I could see that your tower was protected somehow, that the Bluchers weren't touching it. Ours was slowly crumbling beneath us. I hoped – I hoped that you would come for us. You were our very last chance. No one else would come. I couldn't believe it when I heard Obi's voice calling to us from the corridor. It was like a miracle.

'But Evie wasn't ready to go. She didn't want to come with us. She told us to leave her there. But I could never have left her. We made her come with us. She struggled and hit out, she spat in Obi's face. She was crying and shouting. I'd never heard her voice like that before. She sounded like a different person, not like the woman I married. Evie was such a gentle person, she would never have wanted to hurt anybody.

'We got her down to the lower floors, though, and Obi said that he would take her first. We put the oxygen mask on her, and wrapped her up in scarves and anything we had. She wasn't lashing out any more; all the fight had gone out of her. Obi had to carry her. She couldn't stand properly. I watched them leave from the window.

'They made it almost halfway to your tower; they didn't have far to go. But then she seemed to come alive all of a sudden. She started thrashing about and Obi couldn't hold her. I don't blame him. I blame myself. I should have carried her. Maybe she wouldn't have started struggling if I had been holding her. She fell to the ground and she pulled off her mask, pulled off the scarves. That's how she died. Just by breathing in a lungful of the outside air. It only took moments.

'From where I was standing, I could see Obi trying to revive her, but then he had to just take her mask and walk away. He came back to the tower for me. He didn't speak to me when he came back; he just said, "We don't have much time," and then he started getting me ready with Evie's mask and covering my face. He marched me out of the building and across to your tower, but he couldn't avoid us going past Evie on the way, she was right in the middle of where we needed to go.

'She looked like she was sleeping: her hair was spread out from her head like a fan, her eyes closed. She looked sort of lit up from the glow of the Bluchers that were all around her. Lit up. Lit up and beautiful. The last time I shall ever see her, that is how she looked.'

I don't know what to say, but before I can speak, Ben starts talking again.

'I got so mad with Obi when we got here. I started taking it out on him. I blamed all of you. If you'd left us, we'd have died together when our tower fell, and now she's gone and I don't know why I'm still here without her. I couldn't make sense of it. I'm not sure if I ever truly will. But I know now it wasn't anyone's fault. It was just the phobia inside her, it was stronger than I knew. Obi's helped me to start to see that. And I want to thank you, Ade, for finding us in the tower. When you saw my torch and signalled back to us. You gave us our last chance that night. You weren't to know that Evie didn't want it. But thank you. Thank you for trying to rescue us.'

Tears run down Ben's face and fall onto his trousers, making little wet circles, but he doesn't stop to wipe them away. They just keep falling. It is so quiet that I think I can hear them fall. *Plop, plop, plop* they go, each time they splash onto his jeans.

We sit together for a long time, neither of us saying anything at all. Ben's plate of rice lies on the table, untouched, in front of us.

My head feels too full of information, like it is full up now and things are falling out the top of it. I am thinking about how sad Ben is and how sad it is that his wife is not with us now. And I feel funny that Ben thinks I saved him. I was only thinking of Gaia, really; that's who I thought I was rescuing. And when I think about all these things, I can feel tears suddenly appear in my eyes but I blink them away.

I don't want to cry in front of Ben.

I don't know how I can stand up and leave Ben on the sofa crying, but in the end he says, 'You'd better get going. Thanks for bringing the food down.'

I know that he wants me to go.

I don't think I was afraid of Ben before exactly, but I didn't trust him in the same way as I did Obi and Dory. Now that he's told me about his wife and cried in front of me and everything, it's different. I think we understand each other a bit better now. I think I can trust him too.

I get up to leave but before I go out through the door, I turn round.

'Ben, did you know Gaia? She lived on the seventeenth. She had two brothers.'

Ben looks up at me and I can see he is trying to think.

'The family with the three kids? Yes, one girl and two boys. Yeah, I think I know them.'

'Do you know where they are?'

'They packed up and left. Like everyone else. There was no one but me and Evie there, in the end.'

'Oh, OK,' I say. 'See you tomorrow.'

'See you tomorrow, Ade. Sleep well.'

Even though my head hurts from thinking about everything, I can't stop myself from smiling as I walk down the corridor.

I speak to Gaia in my head.

You're all right, I say. *You're all right, you're all right.*

Chapter Thirty-nine

Before I go downstairs the following morning, I look out of the window. I sit up on the windowsill like I used to and press my forehead against the glass.

I don't recognize the view below me. You can't see where the buildings used to be any more or where cars used to drive or where my school playground was. It all looks the same now. I can't even make out the exact space where Gaia's tower once stood.

The space would be completely flat but the trees are still standing. I can see a tall cluster of them in the distance and I wonder if that's where the park was. The trees look very green and leafy and bushy, as if they prefer life without buildings all around them.

The moving silver-blue colour of the Bluchers shimmers. It looks a bit bluer than before, I think. I can see another colour around it now, though. I can see green. Things are starting to grow among the Bluchers, in the places that used to be covered in tarmac or built on with bricks.

We are the only building standing now. The only tower left. I can't decide if the world looks bigger or smaller now that it hasn't got any buildings. In one way, it looks like the ground stretches on and on, but in another way, without the towers and blocks and houses, it's just an empty space. Even the really tall building that looked like it was going to have a point at its very top has fallen now. Someone told me at the time that it was a skyscraper. They hadn't even finished building it after all those months and months of work, but it had still towered over everything else. And now you can't even see where it used to stand.

I draw a picture of our tower block surrounded by the Bluchers in my book, but I get the sizes wrong so the Bluchers look bigger than they are in real life and are as high as the fifth floor.

But when I think about it I'm not sure how tall they are now because I've only seen them from looking down on them, not looking up.

Obi's left some water outside our door, which I put in the kitchen for Mum. Down at Dory's, we try only to use water for drinking and not for anything else. Dory never washes up our plates, for example. She just takes some fresh ones from someone's kitchen cupboards every mealtime. 'Ta-da!' says Dory when she hands us a fresh new plate. There's a flat on her floor which is full of piles and piles of our dirty old plates. There's quite a bad smell in there now and I try to avoid going in as much as I can, but sometimes it's my turn to stack up the dirties, in which case I have to take a really big breath before I open the door and hope for the best. I still prefer that to washing up, though.

I do worry what we'll do if we run out of water. I can't forget the time when the taps stopped working. It feels like a long time ago, but just the thought of it makes my head start to spin again because when I remember, I'm right back there again, lying on the sofa, floppy and sleepy and helpless.

Dory has made porridge for breakfast this morning. It's thick and grey-looking and sticks to the bowl. I'm not sure I'm going to like it.

'You have to smother it with golden syrup, Ade. It's the only way to have it,' Dory says, putting a large spoonful onto her bowl so it's covered with a thick coating of the dark yellow syrup. 'Delicious.'

I do the same, but she says, 'More than that, Ade!' so when I do start eating it, I like it. It's sweet and warm and I finish my bowl quickly.

I go up to one of the flats I haven't looked in yet, to search for food, and I start filling my rucksack, as usual. On the stairs I meet Obi and Ben, who are carrying bottles of water down.

Obi says, 'Good morning, Ade,' as we pass each other but Ben doesn't say anything. He just gives me a little nod and he tries to make his lips smile.

'Hello, Obi. Hello, Ben,' I say.

I think: *Be all right, Gaia, be all right, Gaia, wherever you are.* Every time I see Ben it reminds me that she left. I think hard about her every day, willing her to be all right, wherever she is.

The days pass in much the same way as before Ben arrived. Except he's just there with us, usually helping Obi with something. He eats with us every day now, but doesn't speak much.

He is still very upset. Sometimes we hear him crying.

Sometimes Ben helps me collect food at the end of the day if I can't carry it all, and I realize when he does, how lonely I was before, when it was just me and my backpack and all of those empty, deserted flats.

'That's a good haul today, Ade,' Ben says to me one day as we walk down to Dory's flat, me with my heavy backpack's straps digging into my shoulders and Ben carrying a huge, bright blue bag awkwardly at his side so it doesn't hit his legs.

'How are you doing?' he goes on.

I think about his question. 'I'm OK.'

'It's OK, you know, if you're . . . not,' Ben says. 'It's not easy. Living with someone who's . . . in so much pain.'

I don't say anything but concentrate on walking down the steps, one foot after the other.

'There are good days and bad days. On the good days, you think it might be the beginning of something better, and on the bad days, well, it feels like the world is closing in on you.'

I know exactly what he means, about the world closing in on you. Sometimes the world seems like an impossibly large place, but other times it feels like it is too small and too dark. Like a black cave that has walls which move closer and closer to you with every second that passes.

'You have to believe in those good days, though,' he adds.

I think of the days when Mum used to buy me the big tubs of ice cream, and how they made me forget the afternoons when she wouldn't get out of bed.

They were golden coloured.

I look over to Ben.

'I do,' I say.

'Good,' Ben says.

We don't say anything else on the way down. I feel like we understand each other.

I think Obi seems different when Ben is with us. It's like he's always watching him a bit out of the corner of his eye. It's funny, though, because it makes me sometimes wish that it was back like the times when Ben wasn't here. When it was just me and Mum and Dory and Obi.

I think that if Ben hadn't arrived then I'd be the one helping Obi all day. Not Ben. But I don't like thinking that, so I push the thought away.

One day, though, Ben hurts his back when

he is lifting something. He has to stop working and go and lie down for a while.

I worry a little bit that I might have made it happen by thinking about Ben not being here, because just after it happens, Obi asks me if I'll help him that day instead.

But I forget about this soon enough.

Because at last I find out why the Bluchers aren't able to destroy our tower.

Chapter Forty

Obi takes me down to the basement again. I haven't been there since the day he got ready to leave the tower. The day that I taped the oxygen mask onto his face.

I walk past open doors leading to rooms with bottles and bottles of water stored in them. There are so many of them. I know Obi looks after the water but I had no idea that we'd got so much.

I say as much to Obi but he doesn't say anything back; he just makes a small noise that half sounds like a grunt and half like a sigh.

There's only one thing that's different about the basement now: the swing doors that lead to the bit of corridor with the door that opens to the out-side are sealed shut. There's tape over the crack between where the swing doors meet in the middle and the top of the doors. There's also some kind of fabric which is wedged all along the bottom. As if that isn't enough, there's this huge clear plastic sheet stretching right across the corridor that has been taped to the walls, a little way in front of the doors, so there's not even a tiny gap.

Obi sees me looking at it.

'To keep the spores out,' he explains.

There is another room that has lots of paint pots in it and another that is full of bags of something white and something brown. This is the one we go inside.

When I get closer to it, I read the labels: ROCK SALT, DE-ICING SALT, ICE-BREAKER WINTER GRIT. Bags and bags of the stuff. Piled up almost to the ceiling.

Obi throws one of the larger ones up onto his shoulder to carry in a single swoop. It looks heavy and cumbersome but he starts walking out of the room with it hanging there on his shoulder and I follow. We walk up to about the fifth floor and when we get there, there is a little pile of things sitting in the middle of the corridor.

There are a couple of brightly coloured scarves, a small plastic trowel, like the ones you use to dig soil up in the garden, a bucket and a pair of goggles. Obi puts the goggles on and ties both of the scarves around his face so you can't see any part of it. Just the dark plastic of his goggles sticks out.

He empties some salt from the bag into the bucket and picks up the little black trowel, and it looks like he is about to go into one of the flats when he turns to look at me. It is like he's only just remembered that it is me who has come to help him.

'You need a scarf to cover your face. Go and get one from Dory and come straight back.'

I run up the stairs, and by the time I get to Dory's flat I am breathing so fast it's hard to speak.

But Dory can understand me, even though I am gasping so much. She gives me two scarves which she pulls out of the bottom drawer of a chest.

I run back down to Obi, who is standing exactly how I left him, as if he'd been frozen the whole time I was away.

He helps me wrap the scarves around my face and ties them so tight, I think it's going to hurt. But it doesn't, it just feels quite hot and snug.

'I'm going to go into this flat and I'll be back in five minutes. If I don't come out again, you must not come back in to get me.'

'What do I do?' I ask.

'Nothing. You just go back to Dory and tell her what happened.'

'But what will have happened?' I say. And I can hear that my voice has got a funny little waver to it. It sounds like it's going to break, somehow.

'Well, it means that the spores will have got me, Ade,' Obi says gently.

'But why?' I say. 'Why are there spores in there?'

And that's when Obi tells me how he's been keeping us safe.

Bluchers can't touch salt. They shrivel up and die if they touch it. Obi didn't know it would work at first but it has kept us safe all this time.

He found out about it just after everyone had left us behind, so he wasn't able to tell anyone. No one else knows.

'It won't take them long to find out though,' says Obi. 'Not if an old codger like me could work it out. But everyone's running scared from the spores. They're worried about spreading them around. That's why they stopped flying over, why no one's come to rescue us.'

That's what Obi reckons anyway.

I ask Obi what he does with the salt and he says he just empties it out of the window, all over the bottom of the building. Most of it falls to the ground, protecting us with a circle of salt, but some of it lands on the windows and ledges on the way down. However it's landing, it's working: it's keeping the Bluchers away.

And Obi says it tells us another thing about the sporcs too. Because they aren't flying up and landing and growing on the higher floors. They aren't able to float high up. They're keeping close to the ground, for some reason.

'But how did you know, Obi? How did you know to use salt?' I ask him.

'Well, it sounds a bit far-fetched, Ade, to tell you the truth,' Obi says, 'but when I was your age, my mama used to read to me. Does your mum read to you?'

'Yes.' I nod, thinking briefly how I missed those times. The room would be lit by a lamp, so we could only see the pages of the book in front of us. I'd lean into Mum while her soft voice took us to faraway lands, just by reading about them.

'Well, my mama used to read to me,' Obi goes on. 'Just from one book really. It was the only book we owned. It was full of stories. Stories, stories, stories. So many. My head's full of them.

'There was this one about a man who was so very angry with the people of his city that he salted it. The whole city. As a punishment. To curse it. How did it go again? "And Abimelech fought against the city all that day; and he took the city, and slew the people who were therein, and beat down the city and sowed it with salt." The story went that if you salted the earth then the land became infertile, things wouldn't grow in it. Well, when I was little I couldn't stop thinking about Abimelech: the man who ruined a city just by using something as simple and common as salt! That whole city not being able to grow a single thing to feed it.

'When the Bluchers arrived, it reminded me of Abimelech. I thought, *Would they want to have a city that was salted, that was cursed?* So I covered my face one day and went out there, even with those spores around. I didn't get too close to them but I threw some salt out and some of it hit a Blucher.

It wasn't a direct hit but I'm telling you now, I don't know how, I don't know why, but it worked. It shrivelled right up before my eyes.

'We already had a store of rock salt in the basement for when I grit the pathways in the winter, but I got as many extra bags as I could. And I tried to ring the police and tell them what I found out, but when I finally got through to someone, they just said they would make a note of it and thanked me for my call. I don't think they understood the importance of what I was saying. Or maybe they had a lot of calls like that, people saying they had the answer. Either way, no one wanted to hear what I had to say.

'We don't have to burn them. We just need to salt the earth, and the Bluchers will go. But if I found this out, then someone else will too. And that's when they will come and rescue us. It's just a waiting game, Ade. We won't be here for ever.'

I have never properly thought about someone coming to rescue us. I think a part of me thought that we would always stay in the tower. Me, Mum, Obi and Dory. And Ben as well, now. Had I forgotten how big the world was beyond the tower walls? What it was like to be outside?

Obi tells me that he has to start salting now

and that he will come back out for salt after he has emptied each bucket. Then we'll move on to the next flat along so that he makes sure he goes round the whole tower.

My job is just to help put the salt into the bucket and make sure that Obi comes out of the flats OK. Obi says that he doesn't think that the spores will be flying this high but you can't be too sure, so that's why we both have to wear scarves around our faces. Just in case.

I ask if Ben goes into the flats with Obi but he says that he waited for him in the corridors just like I am going to.

'There's no point risking two lives,' Obi says.

We both pull our scarves tighter over our mouths and Obi goes into the first flat. He gives me his watch to look at, so I can see when five minutes have passed, and then he goes in.

I watch the second hand go round and round the clock but the minute hand never seems to move. Obi's watch is made of metal. I like feeling its weight in my hand. It's smooth and cool to touch.

In the end I give up looking at the hands of the watch and instead I pass it from one hand to the other and I count. On the two hundred and fifty-sixth pass, I hear Obi's voice telling me to close my eyes, and when I say I have, I hear the door opening.

After a few moments Obi says I can open my eyes again, and then we start putting more salt into the bucket and Obi moves to the next door. We do the same thing over and over at every door on the floor until we run out of salt. Then we have to go and get more salt from the room in the basement and keep going until all of that runs out too.

'How do you know that's enough, Obi?' I ask.

'I don't,' he says. 'We'll have to keep an eye on them. See what they do next. If they look like they're growing towards us in the morning, we'll do it again. If the weather stays like this, we'll be all right.'

I ask him what he means.

'Well, we've had dry weather for days and days now. If it starts to rain, then it will wash the salt away. Then there will be nothing to stop them.'

'But it could rain at any time,' I say, thinking of the days and days of rain that leaked from the sky just before the Bluchers arrived. Then I remember those days when you wake up to blue skies and sunshine, and by lunch time there are grey clouds and deep puddles everywhere.

Up to now, we've been lucky with the weather, but it could change at any moment.

'We've got a lot of salt, Ade,' says Obi. 'And remember, someone else will find out that it works against them too.'

I don't say anything, my mind still pondering the heavy rain clouds that until recently had choked our skies.

'Then they'll come and get us. They surely will.'

I know Obi is trying to make me feel better, but his voice sounds a little bit different as he's speaking to me. He's too insistent, too bright, and his eyes look sad although he's smiling with his mouth.

It seems very much as if he is trying to hide something.

Chapter Forty-one

The following morning I climb onto my window-sill and look out to see if the salt is working against the Bluchers. It is. There is still an invisible line that they aren't able to cross.

The sky looks blue. It will be another fine day. *There won't be any rain today, there won't be any rain today.* If I think it enough times, it will come true.

I have been thinking more about Mum. I've worked it out and Mum stopped going out about a year ago, just after the day I found her hurt and crying in the flat.

Ben said that his wife hadn't been outside for seven years. That's much longer than Mum. I can't stop thinking that Mum must be a bit better than Ben's wife was. Maybe she's not as ill as before.

I think if we were rescued then she would

come outside. Also, if she didn't want to come, then there's lots more of us to carry her out. Obviously, there's me and Obi, but Dory would help and I think Ben would too.

She would have to come.

It wouldn't be the same as when Ben's wife had to go outside. I'd make sure of it.

Dory is singing to herself when I go downstairs for breakfast that day. She says we will have something special for dinner tonight but she won't tell me what. It's a surprise.

There's no sign of Obi or Ben. Dory says that they have eaten already and they are doing something with the water tank on the roof. My face must look worried because the next thing she says is, 'Don't worry, you know they'll be careful. And you've heard about Obi's theory that the spores are not flying high over the ground.'

We eat peanut butter on crackers that morning and have a little cupful of tinned fruit each too. I have a funny thing about tinned fruit because I always think it tastes a bit metallic, even when no one else does, so I eat my cup quickly and try to swallow it down without chewing too much.

After I've taken Mum her breakfast I go up to a floor I haven't searched yet, to start collecting more food. The first flat I go into is really smelly and I only find a couple of tins of dog food at the back of one of the cupboards. I don't even have enough food to fill my rucksack, so I go into the next flat along.

Straight away, I can tell that the person who used to live here liked making cakes. There are lots of bags of flour and little red tins of cocoa powder and cartons of eggs and little plastic packets of hundreds and thousands and silver balls.

I stop to look at the photographs hanging on the wall. There is always a pretty woman in each photograph and two little boys. They are younger than me and they have dark, curly hair and big brown eyes. They are smiling in every photo and it makes me wonder where they are now and if they are still smiling as much as they are in the photos.

There are a few photos up in our flat of me and Mum. There's one when I'm a tiny baby and Mum's smiling so hard it looks like her cheeks might crack. There's another one when it's my birthday and I'm sitting on Mum's lap in front of a white birthday cake. They make me feel sad when I see them because things are so different now. There aren't any photos from recently. Everyone knows you don't take photos if you look unhappy in them.

There is too much food to carry from this kitchen, so I start dividing it into piles in front of the window. It will make it easier for Dory when I bring it down.

I put all the flour in one pile and sweet things in another, and in the end I have about seven different heaps of various foods. I will need to take several trips to carry this down.

But just before I start loading it up, something catches my eye from out of the window.

I think I see something move outside.

From behind some of the trees.

It is something or someone just running out of sight to hide. I look again and stare and stare at the little spot where I think I saw something. I see again a flicker of movement in one of the bushes there.

As if someone is hiding just behind it.

I look again and again but I can't see anything more after that. I could convince myself that there is nothing out there but I don't. I keep looking, running my eyes over and over the same patch of bushes, trying to find out what moved there.

I feel sure there is someone there, looking up at the tower right now. Perhaps they have got a mask on like Obi had but are running low on air.

I think: *Maybe they need to come into the tower, just like Ben and his wife did.*

I think: *Maybe they need rescuing too.*

I know I am not a hero. Nothing like a super-hero in a shiny red cape who knows they will save the day. I'm scared and worried and I don't want to die.

And I know I might do if I go out of the tower.

But there is something bigger inside me that makes me turn round and run to the door. There's the feeling I had when I sat next to Ben when he thanked me for giving him and Evie their last chance, and something else as well. It's not a feeling I've ever had before, really. It's just like a certainty that I know the right thing to do, and that is to try and save the person who is out-side the tower.

I know I can't waste any time; I need to go to

them straight away. Ben said that Evie had died in just moments in the open air.

Suppose the person in the bushes doesn't have very much air left? Or perhaps they are injured and can't walk the very last bit of the way to our block?

Suppose this is their last chance?

There is no time to go and find Obi or Dory or Ben. I run downstairs to the basement as quickly as I can. My legs are taking me down the steps so fast that I think they might crumple beneath me at any minute, but I don't fall.

I make it all the way downstairs to Obi's room.

I pick up the tattered rucksack with one of the silver canisters we found all those days ago inside it. The mask is still attached to it. I fiddle with the top of it just like I saw Obi do, and I hear a small hissing sound come from the mask. I put it over my mouth and breathe in. It's working fine. I struggle to put the rucksack on my back. It is too big for me, really, but I can manage it.

Then I start taping up the mask, just like I did when Obi put it on. It's harder now I've got it on myself, and I keep getting the tape tangled so it sticks to itself, and then I have to start again.

Finally I am putting on the old swimming goggles and tying scarves around my face as best I can.

I am ready.

Chapter Forty-two

To get to the outside door, I need to pull down one corner of the sheet that Obi put up and take some of the tape off the swing doors so I can open one.

I feel guilty as I pull apart Obi's protection for us and I try to put it back up behind me. The worst thing I could do is let spores into the tower. It wouldn't matter if I rescued someone, if I managed to kill everyone else while I did it.

I only realize how scared I am when my hands don't seem to be obeying me properly. They seem too big suddenly, and numb, as though I am cut off from them. I swallow and concentrate hard on unpeeling the first of the thick silver lines of tape. I have to tug it hard to pull it off and it makes a ripping sound as it comes off that pierces through me and then settles in a heavy feeling of sickness in my stomach.

I don't know if I'm doing the right thing or not.

I'm not Obi; I don't know what I am doing, I'm just the kid from seventeen.

But I guess there is one way in which I *am* like Obi. When I told him about the lights in the tower, he said that we must try to rescue the people, and that is what I am doing.

I am trying to rescue the person I saw. It's the only thing I can do.

The floor through the swing doors is covered in a thick carpet of grit salt. My feet sink into it so that it reminds me of walking through icy snow, but it looks browny-orange instead of white. Funny how you notice things like that, as though your brain is trying to fool you into forgetting what you are about to do. To lure you into a sense of safety and dismiss the fear that is pulsing through your veins and filling every corner of your mind.

There's more tape on the outside door and most of that needs to come off too. It makes one final screech, a deafening sound that seems to echo down the corridor, but finally I have done it and I pull down the handle and push.

How can I describe what outside looks like

when it is so different from anything I have ever seen?

When I open the door and feel the first rush of air on my face, it feels so cold and startling that it makes me want to step back into the safety of the tower. But after the shock of it, it feels fresh and cool and wonderful.

I'd forgotten about that.

There is a crunching sound as I tread on the salt surrounding the bottom of the tower. It is scattered all about me. I can hear my breath going in and out, in and out. It sounds loud because of the mask I am wearing.

It makes me feel worried how easily one of those tiny little spores might just slip under my mask so I would breathe it in. I must be surrounded by the spores that are floating and swirling all around me but I can't see them at all. It just looks like empty air to me.

Then I come to the Bluchers. In some places they have grown higher than my knees, but in others, they have grown much, much taller and they tower above me. Close up, they look beautiful. And weird as well. As if they are filled with some kind of liquid that is always moving. Swirling around, making circular patterns that are never still.

You can see the inside of them because they have a sort of clear skin which you can see right through. The liquid reminds me of when you see a little puddle of petrol on the road and it has swirls of colours in it. Or when you blow a bubble and it doesn't pop straight away and there's a tiny moment when it is full of moving colours. Pink and green and yellow.

Except it doesn't look like any of those things, not really. It's like nothing else I've ever seen before.

Not like a plant, not like a tree.

When they are fully grown, their stems are as thick as the ropes we used to hang from on the apparatus in our school hall. The rope would feel bulky in our hands when we used to climb up it and most of us could make it to the very top. I don't think you would have been able to climb up a Blucher, though. They look so smooth and shiny that you might slip right down one if you tried.

I have the urge to reach out to touch one of them. They look like they would feel wet and slimy, a bit like jelly. Or like when we used to let snails slide across our fingers if we found one in the playground.

At the top of the stem is a large, roundish

shape that comes up to a little tip. Depending on how tall they are, some of these heads are as small as my finger, but when the stem is really high, they are much, much bigger than my head.

The large ones are swollen and bloated like blown-up balloons, and look like they might pop if you poked them sharply, so I tread carefully, anxious that I will burst one if I hurry past.

Among the Bluchers, all kinds of things are growing.

There are tall, stalky plants that have large, long leaves, and green, bushy shrubs that have little blue flowers on top. Grasses have grown so much that they stand tall and thick, quite unlike the patchy lawns that I knew from before.

These blades of grass look silky and dense, as if they would be difficult to walk through.

I can't understand how everything has sprouted over the buildings that once stood here. There isn't a trace of the homes and shops and roads, not one trace, and when I look down to the ground, I can see that my path is covered in tiny little yellow-green leaves that coat the earth like a carpet.

I dig the heel of my shoe in to lift some away and I see that the soil beneath looks almost black now. It isn't the brown, sandy stuff which would fly from our trowels like dust. It is much, much darker and looks moist and crumbly, like the rich chocolate cake we ate for Gaia's birthday. Only darker still.

I stand among the Bluchers, so shocked by everything I see that I almost forget the reason I am outside in the first place.

The movement in the bushes.

The person who is lying there, waiting to be saved, needing to get to the tower.

I look around at the trees to try and work out which direction I need to go. It all looks so different from what I could see from the window, I can't figure out which bit of green I saw move, at first. It takes me a while, and I have to circle the tower a couple of times before I recognize a craggy branch of a tree which looks a bit like someone's arm bent right over, which was close by to where the person was hiding.

I am not far away from there now and I think I see another rustle in the undergrowth. I freeze, but once again I have the eerie feeling that I might have seen something or I might not have seen anything at all, and now that the moment has passed, I have no way of telling.

My voice is muffled through the mask.

I call out, 'Is there anyone there?' but my voice can't pierce through the plastic of the mask and all the scarves I am wearing. It is trapped beneath the layers.

I can't take anything off, so I creep towards the bushes and keep my eyes fixed on the spot that I think just moved. It's difficult to walk through all the Bluchers as well as all the bristly, wild leaves and grasses that are in my way. I have to move slowly and it takes a long time.

I have just reached the place when I hear someone call out my name from far away. It's a voice I know well: Obi's voice.

I look up to the tower and can just see two tiny little specks on the roof of the block. Obi and Ben. They have seen me. I can't make out their faces but I can hear what they are shouting down to me.

They keep saying the same thing over and over. Louder and louder, each time.

'*Get back inside.*'

'*Get back inside.*'

Chapter Forty-three

It's funny when time slows down or speeds up again.

I've heard people talk about time like that. They say, 'This week is going so slowly,' or, 'Today's rushed by.'

I hadn't really taken any notice of that before.

Sometimes night felt like a long time because I would wake up and think it must be morning and time to get up and have breakfast, and then realize that it was still dark outside and the middle of the night. But I'd never really known time to seem like it had stopped. Not until now, when I am standing outside the tower, with Obi and Ben calling down to me, wearing my air mask, in front of the leafy green bushes.

With the Bluchers all around me.

All of a sudden, Obi and Ben's voices sound

very far away. They get quieter in my head.

I notice that to one side of me is a tall Blucher which is growing next to a patch of the bushes, and then I can't tell what happens first, it all happens so quickly. Or so slowly, depending on which way you look at it.

One moment I am thinking about whether I should try calling back to Ben and Obi that I am all right, and the next, there is just that tiny sliver of time right before something big happens.

It is like the world has just taken a breath.

Do I know it at the time? Maybe I don't.

Maybe I only remember that moment of stillness because of what happens next.

I turn back to look in front of me, and there is a movement in the bushes, and at what seems like exactly the same time, the top of the Blucher right next to me explodes.

Pop. Just like that.

This is the moment that time stops. The little piece of time as I realize that it has burst and the liquid that was in it is now spraying out of it.

Right towards me.

The droplets look like they are frozen, like long thin teardrops hanging in the air. A fountain that I am standing right underneath. And then time restarts again and I feel the wetness of the liquid seeping through my clothes, drenching the scarves that are wrapped around my face.

I can't move. I don't know if I am able to at first.

I stand there, as still as I can, and I can feel the liquid running down my back now and the coolness of it upon my cheeks. I know I am covered, that if this is something that can hurt humans, then there is no chance for me now. But still I am waiting. Waiting for the pain to start, waiting for me to begin to die.

My skin feels a little bit itchy and sticky but I can't decide if I am hurting or not. I start thinking that my skin feels like it is warming up. I worry that it will get hotter and hotter and that soon it will feel like I am on fire. But it doesn't warm up like that. I just stand there, paralysed, waiting for something to happen.

My goggles are coated with the stuff. Everything starts looking a bit blurry through the lenses, although I can still see through them.

What is really strange though is that I can see the colours of the Bluchers through the goggles and that changes how everything looks. It is like

I am looking through a funny magnifying glass which makes everything look hazy and changes their colour. The bush in front of me is no longer green. It seems like it is pale blue now. The little blue flowers are pink, and I can see out of the corner of my eye that the tower now looks almost completely black. It is like a huge, dark shadow looming over me.

I stand there for a long time before I realize that I am all right. I am not hurt.

I can hear Ben still calling to me to get inside. The shouts haven't stopped the whole time. It is just that I have been able to block out the sound in my head.

I know that I need to go back now, but I have come outside to help somebody and I haven't even found them yet.

The bush that moved when the Blucher burst is directly in front of me.

I slowly walk round it and kneel down as best I can with the rucksack on my back, to look underneath it.

There is nothing there.

There are little marks in the dark, black soil that show where something has been, but whatever it is or whoever they are, they have gone.

I look down the only path it could have taken. It's surrounded by swollen Bluchers and thick undergrowth. Trees are growing here, but they are so much taller than I remember and they block out the light.

I suddenly get the eerie feeling that if I go down that path, I won't return.

As I stand in front of the track and decide that I have to go back, I start to feel a little bit silly. I rushed out of the tower to rescue someone and there's no one here. I could have died when the Blucher juice covered me and I risked coming out with spores all over the place and I might have even infected the block with them.

All for something I thought I'd seen.

I turn back to the tower, feeling my shoulders slump. I can hear Ben's voice die down as I turn round and start walking back to the tower. I wonder if Obi will be cross with me for going outside. Will he understand why I had to do it?

And then I start hearing a different noise.

It's coming from down the path. *Pop, pop, pop.* It's the sound the Bluchers make when they explode.

And something else as well. A little mewing noise calling out.

I turn back and I can see the Bluchers are bursting, one after another in a line, right along the path and coming towards me. Something is setting them off.

And then I see it.

It is running away from the sound as fast as it can.

A small, thin cat.

It leaps into my arms as soon as it reaches me and starts purring. It's like it knows I have come to get it.

I turn back to the tower, but as I do so, I feel something stopping me. I look down. It's on my leg. A thin, silvery arm of a Blucher wrapped around my ankle.

And it's beginning to tighten its grip.

Chapter Forty-four

I desperately try to pull my leg away from the Blucher but its grip is crushing. It anchors me to the spot.

I look around frantically, still clutching the cat to me, trying to find any way to escape the Blucher's deadly hold. The Blucher's squeezing me now, so tightly that I wonder if my leg will simply break from the pressure.

I cry out and bury my head in the cat's silken fur. I think: *This might be the end.*

The popping of the Bluchers is so loud that it sounds like the whole world is exploding. Just like when you hear thunder and it seems to make the walls of the room vibrate a little bit. Except I think I can feel the sound in my chest and in my ribs and deep inside my body, in my lungs.

Suddenly I hear a sort of fizz and hiss, and

the pressure on my leg is lessening and lessening. In front of me stands Obi, his face obscured by scarves and goggles, and behind me, I see the shrivelled dead body of the Blucher.

Obi gestures with his arm to follow him and I imagine that if he was able to, he would be shouting with all his might, 'Get inside, Ade, get inside!'

I run to him as fast as I can, although my leg is throbbing and sore. Obi flings open the door of the tower, I run in and he slams it behind me. It closes with a loud bang. I stand with my back to the door until I hear the last of the explosions. And then there is silence.

Obi throws the empty bucket in his hand to the ground and it clangs noisily and rolls and rolls until it comes to a stop. I try hard to slow down my breathing, which is coming in ragged bursts, and I try to take in what just happened outside. It was all down to Obi. He threw a bucket of salt on the Blucher that was attacking me. He saved my life.

Obi pulls off my scarves, pulls off the mask and the goggles. I manage to say, 'I'm OK, Obi, I'm OK,' but I don't think he can hear me because he is pulling off my rucksack and rushing into the little room off the corridor to grab a towel to dry my face with.

The cat jumps down from my arms and now sits by the rucksack looking up at us. I have an awful feeling that Obi is cross with me. It starts in my stomach and it goes all the way up to make a lump in my throat and an ache in my head.

I wait to hear what his first words will be. I am scared he is going to shout. He looks angry and his face is twisted up so much that I can't see his eyes properly.

'What happened?' he says. It's hard to hear him because he's speaking through a scarf which is covering his mouth.

'What happened?' he says again. And I feel the awful feeling leak out of me. He isn't going to shout; he is going to listen.

I tell him about what I saw when I was looking out of the windows. How I thought it might be someone who needed help. That I'd run down to get myself ready to help and that there hadn't been time to go and find him or tell Dory.

I describe how the Blucher burst all over me but how it hadn't hurt and how one of them wrapped a vine around my leg to trap me and that I couldn't find anyone out there in the end.

Apart from just one thing.

And I point to the cat, which is still sitting patiently at our feet, as if it is waiting for the story to turn to it.

Chapter Forty-five

'What are you going to call him, Ade?' Dory asks me as she scratches the pink skin on his tummy.

The cat is lying on his back in a little patch of sunlight on the sofa, in between us both. Dory was delighted when she heard how I'd rescued him.

'You are made of stern stuff, Ade,' she tells me. And she insists on feeding the cat one of our tins of tuna before Obi stops her and says that cat food will do well enough.

Obi sends me off to a couple of flats whose owners used to own cats, and soon I have filled my rucksack with tins of cat food and bags of little fish-shaped biscuits. I also find a litter tray and a sack of tiny white stones to fill it with. The litter is heavy and I have to keep stopping to rest while I am carrying it. I wonder about asking Obi to help me, but even though he didn't shout at me, I think he is still a little bit annoyed that I left the tower and brought back a cat with me, so I don't ask him.

'I'm not sure. What do you think?' I say.

'How about Bluchy?' says Dory. 'Because he survived the Bluchers. He's quite the hero, isn't he?'

'Hmm, how about Mystery?' says Obi. 'Why cats? What is it about him that stops the spores from affecting him?' He looks at the cat suspiciously and then shouts out, 'Oh!' as it jumps right onto his lap.

'Get off! Get off!' says Obi, but the cat ignores him and settles himself down comfortably.

Obi's right. It's odd that the spores didn't kill him. I wonder if there are other animals out there who have not been affected either.

I can't think what he should be called. There are lots of names I could have easily called him, like Smoky or Misty, because he's a soft grey colour, with darker grey stripes from his nose to his tail. But I've always had this funny idea that animals already have names that their mums have given them, and when humans come along and give them a new one, they don't like it very much. I know I wouldn't like being called anything else other than Ade. I think he needs to show me what his name is and then that's what we'll call him. But I feel a little silly telling this to Dory because no one else seems to think it.

'You must name him,' Dory says. 'He's yours now. It will come to you. Look how he follows you around all over the room. He knows he belongs to you.'

Dory starts humming the same tune she was singing this morning and goes into the kitchen to make some tea for us. Even Ben seems to like the cat. He came to Dory's too to see how I was but he hasn't left. He spent a long time tying bits of balled-up paper and corks to a piece of string which he is dragging across the floor for the cat to chase.

It's the first time that all four of us have been together without having a meal to eat before us. There's normally so much to do that we don't really spend time all together, unless we're eating.

My skin still feels a little bit scratchy from the anti-fungal powder that Obi made me put on. It turns out that the little room next to the outside door is where we get 'decontaminated' if we ever go outside. That basically means to get the spores off if there are any on us somehow. Obi wrote it down for me to put in my book when we got back upstairs.

Obi had set up the room just before he went to the other tower where he found Ben and Evie.

First you have to take off all your clothes and put them in a plastic bag which you then put into another plastic bag and then into another bin bag. When you are completely naked and feeling a bit cold by then, you close your mouth and eyes really, really tight and cover yourself with the anti-fungal powder.

I mean *really* cover yourself. All over. And then, when you think you are done and finished, you do it again. I looked as white as anything. By the way, Obi was telling me what to do from outside the room, by shouting through the doorway; he didn't see me do any of this.

Then you have to wait for ten minutes. Just in case. That was the worst bit, because you just want to go home and sit on the sofa or go and have something to eat at this point, but you have to just stand and wait in the middle of the room feeling shivery for what feels like a long time. But it's a small price to pay for not bringing spores in,

I guess, and at least I had the cat with me, who also needed a good coating of powder.

He kept licking it off though, and then shaking his head afterwards as if to say, *This tastes bad but I can't bear to have this powder on me.* After that, you take one of the towels out of the cupboard to cover yourself with and you can come out.

Obi decontaminated himself after me, and while he did that, I went through the swing doors into Obi's room, where he'd told me to help myself to some clothes. They were all far too big of course, but it was just until I went back upstairs to get some of my own.

When Obi was dressed and he had sealed up the doors and the plastic sheet properly again, he decided it was a good idea to salt the corridor floor.

'Just in case,' he said. He was saying those words a lot today. We spent a bit of time pushing the salt over the floor to cover it, and then we came up to Dory's flat, where we've been ever since.

Obi didn't speak to me a lot while we were clearing up the basement.

I wanted to say, 'Are you cross with me, Obi?'

but I couldn't quite bring myself to say the words.

In the end, I just asked him a question. I asked about something that was on my mind, because I thought it might be on his too, and I wondered if that was why he wasn't talking.

'Obi?'

'Yes.'

'Why did that Blucher hold onto me like that? They don't eat humans. So why did it hold onto my leg?'

'Yes, I was wondering about that too,' Obi said. 'I wonder if it had something to do with that little friend of yours.'

'What? Gaia?'

'No, Ade,' said Obi gently. 'The cat. You were holding him when the Blucher attacked you, right?'

I nodded. We both looked at him, playing with his own shadow in a square of sunlight coming through one of the windows.

'Let's have a closer look at him. Go and get him, Ade.'

I went over and picked him up. He immediately started purring into my shoulder. He was such a friendly cat.

'Now, let's see. What's this?'

He fingered a thin, grubby red collar around the cat's neck. He took it off carefully and moved it around in his hands until we could see the little metal buckle.

'I'm not sure, but I think they were after that.'

'But it's so tiny!' I said.

'They're hungry,' Obi said grimly.

We didn't speak about it again.

We spend the rest of the afternoon just sitting in Dory's flat, eating a tin of ginger biscuits that I found a week ago, and playing with the cat. Obi and Ben look really tired for some reason, and they sit slumped on the sofa for quite a while as Dory fusses over the circle of bruising around my leg where the Blucher had hold of me. To take my mind off it, Dory makes us all sit round the table together and play a new card game which she calls Memory.

She lays out all the cards face down on the table, so its entire surface is covered. Then you have to turn over one card for everyone to see and then pick up another to see if you can find the same card in a different suit. If you find a pair, then you take those and put them on your pile.

The game goes on and on.

Ben, Obi and I aren't very good at it and Dory keeps finding all the pairs. Then suddenly Obi starts picking out lots of pairs until he has quite a large pile. And then Ben and I find a few each too.

When we finish the game, everyone gets quite excited about who will pick up the last few cards.

Ben laughs out loud when Obi picks up the wrong card. The cat lies sleeping on my lap, warm and soft. And in those few hours, I forget that only earlier that day, I'd been quite sure that I was about to die.

Chapter Forty-six

That night, we eat well. Dory puts down plates of meat and rice, saying, 'Ta-da!' in a loud, happy voice as she does. It reminds me of the way Gaia shouted, 'Happy birthday!' when she jumped out from behind a tree right in front of me on my last birthday.

We haven't eaten fresh meat like this since the very first time I ate with Obi and Dory. It's the same meat. A bit like chicken, but it looks, and tastes, darker. It has more flavour and is more of a grey-purple colour.

We eat hungrily, and there is the quiet that comes when everyone is eating and enjoying what's in their mouths so much that they don't really want to talk. I like that kind of quiet. Just little sounds of forks and knives on plates and lots of small sighs that mean, *This tastes just great.*

It is Dory who breaks the silence. She can't

help herself. She looks so excited about something that she has to speak.

'Do you like dinner tonight, everyone?' she asks.

We all say, 'Yes, Dory,' and, 'Yes, thank you.'

'Can you guess where the meat's from, Ade?' she says.

I have a think. It's nothing that I've found in another flat and we haven't opened fridges and freezers for meat for a long time.

'No,' I say, 'but we had it the first time I met you.'

Dory claps her hands to her cheeks. Obi smiles.

'So we did!' she exclaims. 'Those were the last ones I had left in the freezer, just after the power went out. But these are fresh ones. Nice and fresh.'

She then turns to Ben. 'Benjamin, do you like it? Do you know where I got it from?'

Ben says that he does like it and he doesn't know.

There's quiet again before Dory starts asking more questions.

'Do you know what type of meat this is, Ade? Can you take a guess?'

I say, 'Chicken?'

Dory shakes her head. Her mouth is in a small, tight smile that makes her whole face crinkle.

'Ben?' she says. 'Do you know?'

He says, 'No, Dory.'

'Ade's cat?' she says, and throws the cat a little piece of meat. 'I bet you know what this is.' The cat sniffs the meat, eats it straight away and looks up, meowing as if he's answering her.

'That's quite right, little cat. That's what it is,' Dory says back to him.

'What kind of meat is it, Dory?' I say.

'Well, seeing as you've asked, Ade, I can tell you that this is none other than the tender breast meat from a lovely, fat, succulent pigeon!' Dory says, beaming.

'But where did you get it from?' I ask. I didn't know you could eat pigeons.

Now Dory looks even prouder and she sits a little taller in her chair. 'I caught it,' she says.

'But how did you catch it?' I ask. 'They always fly away when you go near them.' I remember running past them on the pavement and their soft wings rising up around me like a grey cloud.

'Maybe I could show you tomorrow. We could do with some more,' she says.

She catches Obi's eye and he smiles back at her. As if he knows a secret which we don't.

Chapter Forty-seven

The next morning, I walk down the stairs to Dory with Pigeon following me close behind.

After Dory fed him the piece from her plate last night, he didn't stop meowing for scraps of the pigeon meat, and he even jumped up onto the table when we had finished, to lick the plates.

I wondered if he was trying to tell me that his name was Pigeon, and even though it sounds a bit funny at first, the name fits. It seems to suit him. His grey stripes could be feathers and they are exactly the right sort of pigeon colour.

He seems excited, like me, that we are going pigeon-hunting today. He keeps close to my heels so I almost trip over him, and then he jumps up onto my shoulders where he perches like a bird.

Dory is wearing a flat kind of hat this

morning and she's sitting on the arm of the sofa waiting for us.

'We'll have breakfast later. When we've caught our first one,' she tells us.

She goes into the corner of the room and wheels out one of those trolleys that you use for shopping, just like the one I first used to carry food in from the top flats. 'It's got everything we need inside it,' she says, and gently taps it twice.

'Pigeon is going to have to wait here for us,' Dory tells me.

Pigeon looks at both of us with really big eyes. They say, *Don't leave me here alone.*

I think Dory's thinking the same thing because she says, 'Sorry, Buster, but that's the way it has to be.' She puts some cat treats in a saucer that has little pink roses on it and bits of gold around the rim, and while he's eating them, we leave.

'I wasn't able to risk it for a while because of the spores, you see. Otherwise we could have been eating it all along. We'll wear scarves just in case, but you know Obi doesn't think the spores are able to fly very high, so as long as we go to one of the top floors, we'll be just fine.'

In the end we go to the fifteenth floor and we

find a flat that has an empty balcony. Dory pulls out some scarves that we wrap around our faces. She says something to me but I can't hear her through her scarf, so she makes a little hole for her mouth and says, 'First we need to get their attention.'

She pulls out a clear plastic bag of seeds from the trolley.

'Do you want to come with me? Or wait inside?'

I say that I will come with her. Dory checks something in her pocket and then says, 'Ready?'

She pulls her scarf around her mouth to cover up the hole, opens the balcony doors and we go outside.

As far as we can see there is just the green of plants and the funny colour of the Bluchers. The tops of the trees look like bubbly green clouds, all in different shades, and the patches of thick grasses make odd little shapes among them. There are other colours too, reds and yellows and blues, which must be flowers that have sprung up here and there.

I can't see any pigeons though. And then Dory starts calling to them.

She cups both her hands over her mouth and makes a hooting sound.

Hoo, hoo, hoo.

Over and over.

First one way and then the other. Then she grabs a handful of seed from the bag and gestures to me to take one.

From out of the trees, we see their little grey bodies take to the air and start to fly up to where we are. We hear the sound of their wings beating just before they land in any space they can on the tiny balcony. In the moments before they arrive, Dory throws her handful of seeds onto the floor, and within seconds, each seed has been furiously pecked and eaten.

I throw my handful then, and there is a flurry of movement as they move on to the new lot of seeds. We keep this up for a couple of handfuls each and then Dory passes me the seed bag to hold.

She throws a large scattering of seeds next to one of the walls and then she bends down low straight away. All of the pigeons' backs are to her, pecking away, and then, as quick as a step, Dory picks up a pigeon that is right in front of her. She presses the startled, fat-looking bird to her chest and brings out a bag from her pocket which she puts the bird inside.

Dory throws a last handful of seeds out into the open air, beyond the balcony, and we watch all the pigeons fly off to follow them. When they are all gone, we go back inside.

With the doors firmly shut and our scarves off, Dory opens the bag slowly so I can see its face. She holds it so firmly, it doesn't seem panicked, just mildly curious about what is happening. Dory looks as comfortable holding the bird snugly on her lap as I felt when I was holding Pigeon asleep on my legs last night.

'Good girl, good girl. No need to fret there.' Dory speaks in a low voice which sounds very much like the *Hoo* calls that she made when we first came out onto the balcony.

'How do you know how to do that, Dory?' I ask.

'My father showed me how. It's as easy as pie. You just have to do it quickly. They don't like a ditherer, do pigeons. I must have caught my first pigeon when I was much younger than you are now. Maybe four or five years old. I got my first one in the bag, and I haven't stopped doing it since. Before all this Bluchers business, pigeon meat was pretty much the only meat I ever ate. I'd go down to that little garden bit – you know where there was some grass at the bottom of the tower, call to my pigeons and then, *bam!* Dinner! If only the ovens were working and I could make you roasted pigeon and pigeon pie as quick as looking at you. But the stew's quite nice and you can fry it up. It's not as good, but it's all right.

'People round here used to think I was awfully strange. I am, I suppose. Always feeding the pigeons, you see. They don't like them, they call them flying rats and things like that. Don't know what's good for them. Don't realize it's their dinner flying right past their noses!

'One lady called the police about me – she said that they should make me stop feeding them! I said to them, I'm not breaking any laws, am I? And I wasn't, you see, so they couldn't do anything about it. Just asked me to have a bit more consideration. I started coming down at night after that, so no one would say anything. I suppose some people just don't like them. They feel a bit of fear for them. They can't see how beautiful they are, like this little one here.'

'I like them,' I say. A memory of a grey morning pops into my head then. Of an old woman who was feeding the pigeons at the bottom of the tower. Michael's mum had tutted when we had to walk past. The woman was completely surrounded by birds, with piles of snow-white breadcrumbs scattered over the ground. I had seen Dory before, after all.

'Anyway, enough of my rambling on. It's time for breakfast!' says Dory.

Chapter Forty-eight

The pigeon goes into a cage in Dory's flat where it puffs up its feathers and flattens itself down. It looks a bit like a fluffy ball, sitting there. Pigeon watches its every move, but when he realizes it isn't going to fly away, he comes and sits down at the bottom of the table, by our feet.

We eat porridge again that morning. We are running low on golden syrup now and have to make do with a much smaller yellow blob in the middle of our bowls.

After breakfast, we go back upstairs and Dory catches another two pigeons quite easily. Then she asks me if I want to have a go at catching them.

She shows me how you need to choose the one you want to catch and then you keep your eyes on it so much, it seems like all the others disappear. When that happens, you swoop your arms down and pick it up. Simple.

I don't find it very easy. I keep hesitating about how to pick them up, and they fly away before I can get my hands around them. After about five tries, Dory says I must try and imagine that I am picking Pigeon up instead, and the next time I do it, I get one. It's a little white and grey bird, with black beady eyes.

I suddenly wish I could show Gaia the bird I've caught. I wish she could have seen me swoop down and pick it up and press it close to my chest to stop it from panicking. I know that she'd be good at catching pigeons too.

I'll show her how to do it when I see her again, I think.

But then another thought fills my head: *What if I don't see Gaia again? What if we don't make it out of the tower? What if I can't find her? What if I never see Gaia again?*

The thought makes the world feel like it's tipping over and I suddenly feel sick with the realization that I'll never be able to speak to her again. It's a horrible, horrible feeling.

I can't concentrate on what I'm doing and I loosen my grip on the pigeon I've just caught; and it starts flapping and I can't hold onto it. I let it go and it flies off frantically until it becomes just a tiny dot in the sky. And then it disappears altogether.

'Don't worry,' Dory says. 'Do you want to try again?'

I nod, but I can't catch another one after that. I can't stop thinking about Gaia.

'Let's stop now, Ade,' Dory says after a while. She puts her hand on my back and gives my shoulder a squeeze.

'I think you're missing someone, aren't you? I recognize that face. I see the same one in the mirror when I am missing someone.'

'Who do you miss, Dory?'

'My husband, my children, my mother and father, my sisters and brothers.'

I'm about to ask where they are but Dory carries on talking.

'And then, you know what I realized, Ade? That it was a good thing to be missing someone because that means you really care for them. It means you have love in your life, whether that person is right there in front of you or not. Then I didn't mind quite so much. So whoever it is you are thinking about, you know that all of your love and your caring is travelling to them right now. They'll know it, they'll feel it. They are probably sending it right back to you now, this very minute.'

I don't know what to say back to Dory. I just follow her down the corridor, playing a game in my head where I try to tread in exactly the same places where she treads. I find that I can do it quite easily and if I was winning points for doing it, I probably would have got about a hundred at least.

I used to play it with Gaia but she would get annoyed and say, 'Stop following me around, Adeola, and talk to me properly.' I don't think Dory realizes that I'm doing it, though, because she doesn't ask me to stop.

When we get back to her flat, Dory picks the first bird that we caught out of the cage and goes into the kitchen to fetch a sharp carving knife. We go into one of the flats which we are not keeping food in.

'Have you ever seen anything be killed, Ade?' Dory asks me.

I think about the time I saw a dog run into the road, but when the car screeched to a halt, it walked off, quite unconcerned. I tell Dory that I haven't.

'These days, everyone's kept at arm's length

from the fact that we kill to eat. Unless you're a vegetarian, of course. You can just go into a shop and buy a lovely big chicken – well, you used to be able to, anyway – and you don't have to get your hands dirty at all. It's all plucked and trussed and packaged up and ready for you to bung in the oven. It's someone else's job to kill the animals. We don't see it any more. It's just the way things are these days.

'When I grew up, everyone had chickens and ducks in the garden. Some would even have a goat or a few pigs. It wasn't out of the ordinary. As children, we got used to seeing a headless chicken wandering around. It just meant that dinner was on its way.'

'Dory, why did you see a headless chicken wandering about?'

'Because my mum had just cut its head off, dear Ade. That's one of the ways people killed them back then. But the thing is that their body still moves, so they start flapping about, but they haven't got a head. It's a little bit gruesome. My dad used to say it wasn't very respectful, so he taught me another way to do it. It's quick and there's no blood. Shall I show you?'

I nod.

Dory grasps the legs of the bird with one hand and holds it up so its head is hanging down. She speaks to it in a low voice, but I can't hear what she is saying. Then she puts her other hand around its neck so its head is tilted back a bit. Very quickly, she pulls up with one hand and down with the other.

I'm not sure if I hear it really, but I think there is a sort of *pop*. The pigeon starts thrashing about but Dory just holds it still and keeps talking to it in the same gentle voice as before. It doesn't take long before it hangs quite still.

I come a bit closer to inspect the dead bird. Its eyes are still open but it's quite lifeless. The force that made it flap its wings and peck desperately at our handfuls of seeds is gone.

Where has it gone to? Is it still floating around us, ready to be carried in the wind to another place?

'What did you say to it, Dory?' I ask her.

'Just nice things really. And thank you for feeding us. If someone was killing me for food, I would like them to say comforting things to me. I would like to know that they were grateful to eat me.'

'Yes, I guess I would too.'

We look at the dead pigeon a little longer before Dory puts it down on the table and goes to get the other birds we caught. Each one she treats with the same tenderness and speaks to in the same soft whisper. It doesn't take long before there is just a small heap of their soft, warm bodies.

Dory shows me how to pluck the birds. I am not sure if I want to at first, but once I start, I get quite good at it. Dory calls me Lightning Fingers because I am able to do it quickly. The feathers come out much more easily than I thought. Dory says that is because we have only just killed them. We can make a bit of mess, Dory says, because we can always use this as our Plucking Room from now on. Little grey feathers float all around us in the air and settle onto the carpet like snow.

After that, Dory shows me how to cut off the bit of the wing that you don't eat and she carefully cuts out two bits from the body of the bird which she says is called the breast meat. The meat looks rich and dark purple-red.

'Look at all the goodness in this, Ade,' Dory says. 'This will keep us going.'

There is one last thing to do, which is to get rid of the parts that we aren't using and all the feathers that we have plucked. Dory says they've come from the air, so that's where we'll put them back.

We throw them up, up, up into the light blue sky, from the balcony.

For just a few seconds, the bodies of the birds look like they are flying before they plummet down to the bottom of the tower.

But the feathers drift slowly down. Like a swirling grey storm.

Chapter Forty-nine

I think Mum likes the pigeon meat.

She had started leaving bits of food on her plate that she didn't like, but she never leaves any pigeon. I've been out of the flat so much in the day, collecting food or helping catch pigeons, that when one day I come back in the morning, I'm surprised to find her standing at the big windows in the sitting room.

I go up to stand beside her. I can see my scrapbook is open on the table, not where I left it tucked under my pillow, so I guess Mum must have been reading it. It's been left open on the page where I wrote down:

How to Kill and Prepare a Pigeon. Instructions and Illustrations.

Neither of us speak; we just stand there

looking out. Everything outside has grown bigger and lusher and greener. The sun lights up the Bluchers, making them stand out. They are everywhere.

Mum speaks first. Her voice sounds a little bit raspy and she has to clear her throat a few times before she can speak clearly.

'Why's our building still standing?' she says in a small voice.

I try to explain about the Bluchers and the salt and the spores which aren't landing higher up on the building and that we've been lucky with the weather because there hasn't been any rain for a long time so the salt hasn't been washed away.

I realize that I sound a little bit like Obi, that I'm saying everything just like he would do. I finish off by saying that if we could work it out about the salt stopping them, then someone else will too and that's when they'll come and rescue us.

'How do you know all of this?' she asks.

There's so much to tell Mum that I don't know where to start.

Should I tell her about the other day, when I went out into the middle of all the Bluchers and one of them burst all over me and I thought I was going to die?

Or perhaps I should start on the day when I first met Obi and Dory and we all sat down together around the little red-and-white checked table and ate pigeon, even though I didn't know that's what it was at the time?

Or maybe I should go right back and talk about the day when they closed the school, and how I never said goodbye to Gaia, and Michael's mum tried to take me with her so I barricaded the front door shut?

All this time, Mum's been sleeping or sitting in her room, hiding herself away.

I wonder if I look different to her. Older. Taller, perhaps. Is there something to show for everything that I've seen and done since we've been trapped in the tower?

Mum looks just the same to me, except that her hair is a little longer. She's got the same kind face and brown eyes that look like they are smiling. It's like nothing much has changed because she hasn't been doing anything different than she was before the Bluchers came. She hasn't stood in front of one and seen how tall and silvery it is. She's never spoken to Obi or

Dory. She hasn't seen Ben crying in front of her. She's just the same. She hasn't changed.

Have you ever looked at someone for so long it seems like their face starts to change right in front of you? Their eyes might get smaller or their mouth seems larger or their nose looks like it's growing outwards somehow? That's what happens when I'm trying to answer Mum that day. Her face seems to go all funny and distorted and I forget it's Mum I'm looking at. It's just pieces of somebody's face. It could be anyone.

'What's happened, Ade?' she says. 'Are there many of us left?'

It is a weird feeling that comes over me then because really this is what I wanted Mum to do from the very beginning, but now that she is awake, standing in front of me and asking questions, I feel sort of strange.

Mostly I am glad because it is much better than her just being asleep all the time, but I also feel something else too. Something a lot like anger.

I remember the times before Mum stopped leaving the flat. I have a memory of us sitting on the grass outside together, and though I can't remember where we were or what we were doing, I know that we were happy. In my head, it was a sunny day.

I remember Mum walking me to school and I can picture us going to the shops together and eating in a restaurant, like other people do sometimes. But there's too many other memories clouding out the good ones from before. Memories of her sleeping in her bed, her back to me. Or me taking out empty plates and cups from her bedroom and refilling them again. That's what I think of, mostly, when I think about Mum.

I say something that I used to imagine saying all the time. So much that I stopped thinking it long ago.

I say, 'If you come out of the flat with me, I'll tell you what happened.'

If you come out.

If.

Chapter Fifty

Mum looks at me hard for a moment or two.

'All right, Ade,' she says.

And it's as simple as that. I open the front door and she peeks her head out of the doorway and looks down the corridor, and then she walks right through it. She follows me down the stairs.

She's slower than I am and I have to keep stopping so she can catch up. We stop and look out of the windows at each floor.

'It's all gone,' Mum keeps saying, over and over. 'Can you believe it, Ade? It's all gone.'

We start to play a little game. It's Mum's idea. We close our eyes and pretend that everything is how it was before and say out loud what we can see.

Mum says, 'I can see a plane going over in the sky,' and I say, 'I can see the tops of the buses

279

with numbers on them,' and Mum says, 'I can see the City,' and then Mum counts down from three and we open our eyes.

Everything that we saw with our eyes closed vanishes and is replaced by the silvers of the Bluchers and the greens of the plants and the trees. We play it a few times, and each time, it surprises me when I open my eyes. Mum's making me remember what it used to be like.

I think I had begun to forget a little bit.

We get to Dory's front door and I knock on it, which seems a bit odd because usually I just walk in and call out to her, but it feels different with Mum with me. I hear Dory's footsteps come to the door, and then she opens it with a big smile.

'Come in, come in,' she says. 'It's lovely to see you.'

She bustles us into the sitting room, and in no time at all we are all sitting down with cups of hot tea in our hands, chatting away, as if we have always done this. Dory and Mum talk about everything that has happened and about how Obi's been keeping us safe, not only with the salt he puts down but with the water that he rations out.

Mum asks Dory if she thinks we'll be rescued soon.

'There's no doubt, dear,' Dory says. 'No doubt. Who knows, they might be on their way right this minute.' And she winks at me.

I tell Mum a bit about the pigeons that we've been catching and how I can do it now. Dory is just saying, 'You have a fine young man there,' when, quite suddenly, Mum puts her cup down on the table so it makes a bit of a rattle and says that she'd better be getting back upstairs.

She gets up to leave too quickly and she bangs her knee on the table; She looks like she might be sick or something; her face looks like it's lost its colour.

She doesn't wait for me to come with her.

She walks straight out of Dory's flat without saying goodbye.

My ears feel hot and red and I don't know where to look. I hope Dory likes Mum even though she left so suddenly and didn't say thanks for the tea or anything.

When I finally look up, Dory's looking right at me and she says in a soft voice, 'You do understand, don't you, Ade, that I think your mum's a brave woman? I hope she comes to visit again, if she'd like to.'

I don't know how to answer Dory because I'm not sure how to tell her that I don't think Mum will ever come downstairs again.

Chapter Fifty-one

The next morning, though, when I go into Mum's bedroom to collect her dinner plate, she's not there. She's not anywhere in the flat. Not in the corridor. Not on the stairs.

I call out her name and Pigeon follows me, making loud meows as if he's calling out to her too.

Muu-um, Muu-um.

I can't find her.

I've never before not known where she is, and it scares me.

What if she went outside the tower? What if she didn't believe what Dory and I told her about the spores?

I run down to Dory's so that everyone can help me look for her, but I come to a stop before I push open the door. I can hear Mum's voice in there. And Dory's. And Obi's and Ben's.

The only voice that is missing is mine.

When I go inside, everyone is sitting down to breakfast like we do every day. Except there's an extra chair for Mum. They all say, 'Good morning, Ade,' and, 'Did you sleep well?'

Mum reaches across to me and ruffles my hair, and she looks good. Not sick like she looked yesterday.

She doesn't stay for very long that morning but she comes back to eat dinner with us. The next day she does the same. And the day after that she helps Dory and me pluck the pigeons for dinner and stays with Dory while she cooks.

No one mentions the time when they didn't see her. No one talks about how they're glad she's come out of the flat. They are just pleased to see her each time she turns up.

After only a few days, it seems normal to find Mum helping Dory or Obi with something or other and having an extra place for her at the dinner table. Sometimes she still has to rush off very suddenly, but she'll come back a few hours later.

One day, I come downstairs with some supplies and I overhear her talking to Dory through the open door and something about the way she is talking stops me from walking in. I stand still and I listen.

'I didn't see their faces,' she is saying.

'My dear,' says Dory. 'I can't imagine.'

'There were five of them.'

'Five? Against one? What must they have been thinking?'

'They didn't think, Dory. They just punched and punched and kicked and . . . I didn't think . . . I didn't think I would get away.'

'But you did, my dear. You did.'

I accidentally drop one of the tins I was carrying, and they stop talking and Dory comes to the door to help me. Mum smiles when she sees me. Her eyes look bright but she's not crying.

I worry that she must feel tired because she's not getting the same amount of sleep as she did before, but when I ask her that, she laughs out loud and says that she's not tired at all, that she feels better than she has done in a long time.

I can scarcely believe how much better she is; I keep thinking that there'll be a day when she won't get out of bed again and this time she has spent with Dory, Obi and Ben will just have been a dream I had once.

I keep waiting for that day to come. I wait and I wait but it doesn't happen.

And just when I start thinking that Mum really *is* all right, that's when the rain starts to fall.

Chapter Fifty-two

The first time I hear it, I am lying in bed at night. I am half sleeping, half dreaming when the sound of the rain wakes me.

It takes me a few minutes to realize what it is. It's such a soft sound if you really listen to it, the pitter-patter of the rain, but to me that night, it sounds deadly. Terrifying.

I pull back the curtains. The sky is clouded over but it is beginning to get light outside. The rain is falling steadily down onto the green on the ground. Onto the swelling Bluchers below.

I try to look down at the bottom of the tower to see if they have started to grow towards us but I can't make anything out. It all looks blurry through the rain.

Pigeon wakes up when I start moving and I pick up his sleepy body so he hangs over my shoulder. He feels heavy and warm against me.

When I put him down, he settles right on top of my legs so I can't move them.

In the end, I just pull the covers over my head to try and block out the sound of the rain and go back to sleep.

All I can do is wait for morning. And hope that it has stopped by then.

But in the morning, the rain is still falling.

The clouds look darker now. They are bigger, more menacing. Puffed up and heavy with the rain they are carrying.

I have a feeling of dread in my stomach. I know the rain could stop and we might be all right. I know that people could be coming to rescue us at any time. But I also know that both of those things might not happen. That this could be the end for us now.

And there is nothing that Mum or Obi or Dory or Ben or I can do about it. Our tower will fall down and we will be trapped inside it.

I walk slowly to Dory's that morning. Pigeon is balancing uncertainly on my shoulder and rubbing his ear against mine now and again. It feels like he is saying, *Keep going, keep going.*

There's no one in Dory's flat when I get

there. Not a trace of anyone. Not a half-empty cup of tea or a plate of crumbs on the table. Just silence.

I know where I will find them all. I start the long walk down to the lower floors and find the one where I helped Obi pour the salt out of the windows. I can't see anyone there, but there are bags and bags of salt piled up in the corridor.

Then a door opens and Obi comes out of one of the flats, his head wrapped up in scarves. He doesn't see me. He just picks up another bag and goes into another flat. He looks tired. His back is stooped and his shoulders slump as if there is a large, invisible weight pressing down on him and making him bend. The door slams behind him and echoes loudly down the corridor.

Then I hear footsteps on the stairs and I see Ben coming up, carrying more bags of salt. His face is sweaty from climbing the stairs and carrying the bags. He doesn't seem to have time to talk to me properly, but he tells me to go and help downstairs in the basement.

Pigeon and I make our way down. Through the lower windows, I can see that more and more

Bluchers have surged up. They have grown taller and thicker and they are growing so close to one another, it seems like they are trying to push each other out of the way. The rain falls on their glistening bodies so that they look even shinier than before. They look so glassy now that I think you might be able to see your own reflection if you stand before one.

I look away from them, but then a slight movement at the corner of my eye makes me quickly glance back.

Have I just imagined it or do they look bigger than they did just a moment ago? Are they growing in front of my eyes?

They stand tall and proud, and though I can't see them moving again, their stillness seems even more frightening. It is as if they are waiting until I have turned away before they move forward. I know that is quite impossible but it is how I feel that morning as I stand staring at the shiny, sharp tips and engorged, thick bodies.

I find Dory and Mum in the basement. They are both kneeling on the ground doing something, but they stand up when they see me and hug me tightly to them.

'Are you OK, Ade?' Dory asks me. 'We knew

this day might come, didn't we? We'll be all right, though, don't you worry. Your mum and I are spreading salt into all the corners of the walls and around every window. Can you give us a hand?'

We work all day, pushing the white salt granules into every little crack and corner that we can find in the basement. It takes a long time to do it properly. My fingers feel sore and raw by the afternoon, my hands have turned red, and there is still so much to do. Pigeon stays close to us all day, watching us work and looking out of the window. Dory says that he is our lookout.

We don't stop properly to eat that day. All of us just keep going until we get really hungry and then we go off and quickly find something to eat, and carry on working as soon as we have finished. I only have time to eat a Snickers bar and some cheese crackers which have turned a little bit soft from being open too long.

Dory makes us all stop for dinner that evening, though. She lights lots and lots of candles so that the room is full of their soft, golden light. We eat bowls of sticky rice which has mushrooms in it. It's creamy and easy to swallow.

'Shame we couldn't have pigeon today, folks,' Dory says. 'I ran out of time. But I'd been saving this packet of mushrooms for a while now.'

I notice that Obi doesn't tell Dory off when she opens a large tin of tuna for Pigeon. In fact, he hasn't really spoken much today.

There are a few moments, while we are all eating our food, when, if you were looking at us sitting around the table enjoying our dinner, you would not have been able to tell that we are on the very edge of disaster. That while we are pushing forkfuls of soft rice into our mouths, the Bluchers are creeping around us in a deadly circle, ready to eat the stones and bricks of our home.

But it doesn't last very long, and as soon as our bowls are half empty, everyone starts talking about what we have done today. And what we should do next.

Mum and Dory say that the basement has been salted so they will move on to the next floor up now. Obi says that the Bluchers haven't moved much further in today, but as soon as we stop putting salt out they will come closer. The rain is washing it away as fast as they are laying it.

Ben suggests that we should keep throwing salt out of the windows through the night, in shifts, which everyone thinks is a good idea.

Then Obi voices something that everyone is worried about but no one has said anything about yet. That we haven't got a lot of salt left now. That we are down to the last of the bags.

'I can find some more,' I say. It's the first time I have spoken and everyone turns to look at me. 'I know where to look, from going to find food all those times.'

'Ade,' Obi says. 'That would be brilliant.'

Suddenly it seems that there isn't even enough time to finish our dinner, there is far too much to do. The night coming is no reason to rest.

We leave our half-eaten bowls on the table, our forks still resting in them, and get back to work. Pigeon won't leave his food, though. He protests so much when I pick him up that we leave him in Dory's flat.

The rain has continued to fall heavily all day and shows no sign of stopping as darkness falls around us. It is just like the time when the Bluchers first showed up, when the first buildings tumbled. The rain which never stopped falling, which started it all.

We all have to work by torchlight now. Mum, Obi, Dory and Ben go downstairs to continue the salting, but I go to the upstairs flats, to look for salt.

I haven't been out and about in the tower when it's so dark before. Without Pigeon wrapping his furry body around my legs or perching on my shoulder, I feel something that is a little bit like being afraid mixed with the quiet of being alone. And things look different in the dark. They look like they could be something else entirely.

My mind is bubbling away with ideas of what things could be, but I keep returning to the same image of the tangled bodies of the Bluchers, stretching out slowly towards me.

I know I won't be any help to the others if I keep thinking about these things, so I try to concentrate on them instead.

I think about Dory's wrinkled, serious face when she's playing cards, and how Obi's body always sags when he is sad about something so I can always tell. I think about Ben telling me how he'd never forgive himself for his wife dying, with trails of tears running down his face.

I think about Pigeon's thin grey body leaping

from the exploding Bluchers and into my arms. I think about Mum's face lit up by candlelight, as she sits quietly with us, eating dinner, and then reaching across the table to ruffle my hair, with a smile.

And I think about Gaia too. I think, *I want to see her again.* And I think, *I wish I'd had the chance to say goodbye.*

If it doesn't stop raining and we don't find enough salt, all these things will be lost. They will just vanish. Into the air. And no one will ever know them.

No, that's not quite right. They will be crushed. Devoured by Bluchers.

If someone comes to look for us in a few days' time, they won't even be able to find where our tower once stood. It will just be covered in clumps of glowing, hungry Bluchers growing ever taller and more tangled.

I give my head a shake because I realize now that it's far too important to try and save them. I don't waste any more time being scared of things that aren't there and that my mind is just trying to make up to scare me with.

I fling open front doors and cupboard doors and find every little bit of salt that I can.

Sometimes I am lucky and find clear plastic bags full of salt or largish bottles of table salt. Other times, I only find little glass salt shakers which are half empty.

It doesn't matter, though. We need every little bit, every last grain. I make piles of what I find on each floor in the corridor by the stairs so the others can come and take it when we need it, and I work my way down the tower.

Floor by floor, flat by flat. Shaker by salt cellar.

When I reach my own flat, I stop to sit down.

I think, *Mum hasn't come back, they must be still working, I should go down and find them.* But the flat is so still and quiet, apart from the non-stop dripping of the rain falling outside, that it makes me want to be still and quiet for a minute. So I just sit there.

I don't mean to lie down or close my eyes, but I feel a great weariness take over me. It feels just like a wave going over my head, or as if someone has just pointed a wand at me and said, 'Sleep.' I want to sleep and I can feel my head pulling me down, but at the same time, I don't want to just yet, as tired as I am.

I take up my usual position on my windowsill

and, in the darkness, look out of my window. I shouldn't be able to see anything, because there aren't any street lights any more.

But I can.

As my eyes grow used to the dark, I can see every Blucher, their spiky tops all pointing upwards. Drinking up the rain. Just like how Gaia used to lift her face to the sky. And the reason I can see them is because they are all giving off a little glow. It's not a strong light; it's a bit like those stars that you can stick to your ceiling that glow in the dark, maybe not even that bright. But it's light enough that by sitting there at my window for a little while, I can see them.

What I notice next is stranger still. I realize that the trees themselves are giving off a glow too. It's not as bright as the light from the Bluchers but it's there nonetheless. And if I look even closer I can see the glow coming from the grasses and the bushes on the ground. From all the plants that are not Bluchers.

They are all connected now. They have become part of the Bluchers and the Bluchers have become part of them.

It makes my head feel dizzy to see the whole world glowing like that. Because as afraid as I am of the Bluchers and as sad as I am about all the people who have died because of them, looking at them tonight, I still find them beautiful. And now the trees and the grasses and the bushes are part of that beauty too.

A small voice in my head wishes that we could both exist together, that the spores didn't catch in our throats and kill us and that we lived in wooden houses that they wouldn't feed on.

It's a silly thought though and as soon as I think it, I dismiss it.

As if I'm blowing out the candles on a birthday cake.

Chapter Fifty-three

There's no time for sleeping. And from some-where in my head, a line of a poem pops out. I don't feel like I can understand poems most of the time, but this one has stayed with me for a long time. Well, one line of it anyway. It's some-thing like: *And miles to go before I sleep . . . miles to go before I sleep.*

I'm not even sure exactly how long a mile is. Is it as long as a corridor in the tower? Or is it more like the length of ten double-decker buses? It's probably longer. Miles and miles. It sounds like a long way. Walking down to the basement that night, it feels just like that. Miles and miles.

And then I am there and I am about to shout out to the others, and I can hear their voices talk-ing, talking through the doorway, and then I hear something that stops me. Someone laugh-ing. It's a weird sound that bounces off the dark walls and I can't understand why someone would be laughing when we are all in danger.

Then I hear Dory's voice.

'Stop crying, pet,' she commands, not unkindly. 'We need to think about what to do. We need a new plan. We can't give up all hope. Not yet. Think of Ade. We are going to get him out of this, if it's the last thing we do.'

I turn the light of my torch off and I don't move. I flatten myself against the wall and listen in the darkness.

'They're in the building, Dory,' Ben is saying. 'What else can we do? The spores are in the air. We can block off the lower floors but they're going to take over soon.'

'Ben's right,' Obi says. 'We haven't got enough salt left now. All we can do is try and use the salt we have left on the one coming up the drain and then move further up the tower and then – then . . .'

'Wait to be rescued. They'll come. They'll come. Did you listen to the radio tonight? Did they mention it?' Dory says.

'There's a meeting about it tonight, I think. But they don't think there are any survivors. They don't know we're here,' Obi says.

There's a long pause then, where the only sound is Mum's cries. They are getting quieter now, though.

'I'd better get the mask on and salt that Blucher,' Obi says. 'Coming up the water pipes.' He gives a little almost-laugh. 'I didn't see that one coming.'

And then Mum says, 'But the spores are through there, Obi. They'll be in the air now.'

I can imagine Obi turning to her, as he once did to me. Back when I told him that I'd seen lights in the other tower and I thought Gaia was in there.

'We must try to stop them,' he says. 'We must try for Ade.'

I walk away then, as quietly as I can, spreading my weight across my soles like I used to when I played the Silence Game, and I move noiselessly down the corridor, back to my flat.

I don't want them to know that I heard everything they said.

Despite everything, I can't help feeling cross that they didn't tell me they had a radio all along. It's difficult to explain why, after what I have just heard – even that the Bluchers have come up through the water pipes into the tower – I mostly feel upset about that.

And left out, I guess. Left out. It's yet another thought I've had tonight that I need to unravel from my fingers and let fall to the floor. Because the other thing that I've overheard is how far they'll go to protect me.

And it's weird because it seems like, from their voices, they want to save me more than they want to save themselves. Even though they can't, really, and Dory still believes for no reason that we will be saved, and Obi's going to go into a room with spores in the air just to give us a last chance to survive this.

And I hang onto that thought and it makes me want to cry, but mostly to never forget that this is what people do for each other.

Chapter Fifty-four

Obi said we were almost out of salt, so I go back to the upper floors and start collecting up the piles I made into a bin bag. When I fill one up, I start the journey downstairs again. It takes both my hands to carry it.

'Ade! Ade!' I can hear Mum running up the stairs, calling out to me. 'Ade! Ade!'

'I'm here, Mum,' I shout down, and she runs up to me and hugs me so tightly that I think she's going to break me.

'Something's happened,' Mum says. 'There's a Blucher in the water pipe – they're in the building.'

I can see where her tears have dried on her cheeks and the little white smudges where she has tried to wipe them away.

'We need to get a mask on you,' she says. 'Just in case.'

'What do you mean?' I ask. 'We've only got two masks. Why do I need to wear one?'

'Come downstairs and we'll explain what we're going to do,' Mum says.

I don't want to wear a mask.

I know what Mum means: they want to make sure I'll be OK by giving me a mask. But I won't wear one when it means the others can't.

I don't want them to protect me any more. I want to help them.

'I'm not going down with you, Mum,' I say.

She looks shocked, as if I have slapped her around the face. I realize it's the first time I've ever said I won't do something she's asked me to do.

'You need to take this bag of salt down to the others while I collect the rest of it.'

I hold the bag out towards Mum. She hesitates.

'We need this salt, Mum. Take it down to them and I'll come down with another bag when I've collected it.'

'No,' Mum says. I'm about to start pleading with her when I see a small but distinct twinkle in her eye.

'No,' she says again. 'I'll come back up for

the next one.' And she gives me a look that is not quite a smile but could almost be one.

She takes the bag and starts running down the stairs with it. She looks like she might fall over it and the bag bangs against each stair as she drags it alongside her. I have to get moving.

I run back up to fill another bag with the salt I found. There isn't enough to fill it completely, so I'm back to going through people's cupboards. I knock chairs over that I don't see in the dark and I yank open doors, but I'm not able to find very much in people's kitchens any more and I wonder if it is because I am not looking properly now, I'm panicking.

I remember what Dory said about missing someone, about it being a good thing because it shows that you care for someone. But it doesn't feel like a good thing that I won't see Gaia again. It feels like a knife through my chest.

I'm looking and looking for packets of salt or salt cellars, and tears run down my face. *I don't want it to be the end*, I think. *This can't be it, can it? I can't believe I won't see Gaia again.*

I grab at boxes and jars, but the tears have blurred my sight so I can't read their labels.

Chapter Fifty-five

'Ade, it's not up for discussion. As soon as we see the first crack you're putting the mask on and you're getting out of here. As far as you can go. You keep walking, run if you can, you don't stop. Do you hear?'

Obi's talking and talking at me but he's not looking at me. He's walking up and down the room in front of me and talking to his feet.

'When you see the rescue helicopter, you take these fireworks and you put them in the ground and light them with these matches and then run away as far as you can until they've stopped exploding. The helicopter will find you then. OK?'

Obi's packed up a bag with fireworks and some food for me, and also the rucksack with the silver oxygen canister in it. We only have one left now because the other one is empty after my adventure outside when I found Pigeon, and Obi used the last of it to go into the basement to kill off the Blucher in the water pipe.

Ben and Mum are pouring the last of the salt out of the windows so it's just me, Obi and Dory again. Just like on the first day I found the water.

'Dory, can you tell him?'

I won't answer Obi's questions. I can't leave the tower without them. I won't.

'Ade,' Dory says. 'Ade, please look at me when I'm talking to you.'

I look up at her kind, familiar face.

'Do you know why Obi and I didn't leave the tower when everyone else did?'

'No,' I say.

'Well, it was because of you. We knew about you. And your mum. And when you didn't leave, we decided that we might as well hang around too. We didn't care about the Bluchers and what might happen to us. Look at us. We don't get these wrinkles from doing nothing. Obi and I have had great, great lives, and they've been made all the greater by knowing you at the end of them. You must leave this tower by yourself, dear Ade. I know it's not what you want, but you must try to give yourself this one last chance. It's what we all want. Me, Obi, Ben – and your mum most of all. I know there's someone out there you are missing. I'm right, aren't I? There is someone. You must go to them now. We can't go with you. I'm so terribly sorry that we can't. There's only one oxygen tank left now and it's yours, Ade. It's meant for you. I know you can do this, Ade, because there's someone out there you are missing and it's time for you to go to them now.'

I feel a great weariness coming over me. A heaviness that pulls on the back of my eyeballs and down on my throat. I hear someone gasping and then I realize that it's coming from me.

I cry and I cry.

And I realize that I must go.

Chapter Fifty-six

'That's all of it gone,' Ben says when he and Mum return.

I see Dory give Mum a small nod as she comes in, and Mum runs to me and gives me another one of those hugs that feels like it might break me.

'You're going to be OK, you're going to be OK,' Mum says. She speaks into my head as she's holding me and her voice sounds muffled but I can hear her start to cry as she says it.

'We haven't got long,' Obi says, and he looks out of the window at the tracks of rain running down the glass.

Obi helps me put the rucksack on and Mum takes off the scarf that she was wearing for me.

I know soon I'll have to put the mask on, and no one will be able to hear what I'm saying, but I don't really know what to say while I can still speak.

I don't know how to say goodbye.

In the end, I don't have to worry about that at all.

Just as Mum places the scarf around my neck, the walls of the room start to move around us.

Obi grabs the mask and pulls it over my mouth and starts to tape it up. He doesn't look me in the eye, he just looks at the mask he is covering with tape. Then he ties the scarf around my face tightly so just my eyes are showing.

Pictures fall from the wall and smash on the floor. I close my eyes. Is the tower going to fall? Is this the end?

'Good luck, kid,' I hear Obi say.

The shaking has stopped. We aren't crashing to the ground. I'm not sliding across the floor in a heap. Obi presses a torch and the bag of fireworks into my hand, and I hear Ben shouting, 'Goodbye, Ade!' over the din. Mum grabs my hand and pulls me to the door.

'Go well, dear Ade,' I hear Dory say.

Mum pulls me into the corridor and towards the staircase.

'There's no time, darling, just go,' she says,

and she pushes me towards the stairs. 'You go from here.' Her words are choked with tears but I can understand her.

'Go now, go!' she shouts.

I turn my back to her but I hear the last thing she says before the doors swing shut behind me.

'Know that I love you, Ade. I really love you.'

Then the doors shut and I really am on my own.

Chapter Fifty-scven

I can see cracks in the walls as I walk down to the lower floors. They are thin and long at the moment, like spider webs, but I feel like I can see them widening before my eyes.

My head hurts. I want to turn back but my legs carry me all the way down to the basement. I go past Obi's little bedroom and pull the plastic sheets down from the doors. I almost feel like I'm a robot, doing these things. I don't think about them too much, I just do them.

Then I am there, right in front of the door which will take me outside, and without hesitating I put my hand on the handle and push it open. There's something in front of the door so I can't get it fully open.

It's a tall, shiny Blucher, leaning right into the tower.

I edge past it and squeeze through the narrow opening.

I am surrounded by Bluchers. They have grown so thick it's hard to find a path through them.

I have to force my way through, looking for gaps and finding holes, but I feel trapped, surrounded.

I am in a forest of Bluchers and there is no way out.

Then I hear a sound I haven't heard in a very long time.

It takes me a moment to remember what it is.

It is a bit like a heartbeat. Steady and strong. But much faster and louder.

The sound of a helicopter. Close by. Just above.

They have come to rescue us, just as Obi promised, just as Dory hoped.

I look up and I can see it! It's real!

It's hovering just by the top of the tower and it is waiting there. It is waiting for us to get to the top, to get into the helicopter, to rescue us.

I quickly turn round towards the tower, but I can't see the door any more. It's hidden behind the thick clusters of Bluchers, which are hungrily feasting on our building.

I can't see how to get back.

I don't know the way.

Chapter Fifty-eight

'Follow my voice, Ade,' Gaia said. 'I'm over here.'

We were playing a kind of Blind Man's Buff, but it was a much nicer version where kids didn't push you about all the time. It was only me and Gaia playing it and I just had to try and find her by following the sound of her voice.

'Ade, Ade, I'm over here,' Gaia said again, and I walked uncertainly in that direction and put my hands out in front of me.

I felt something solid.

'Yes, you've found me,' she said, and pulled the blindfold from my eyes so I could see her smiling face . . .

As I stand there, looking for the door, I think I can hear someone calling my name. I move towards the sound, and I push past a tall Blucher in my way.

I stop and listen. I hear it again.

I weave past another few Bluchers and stop again.

I can definitely hear someone saying my name and I move again in that direction.

Finally, I see the black door and I squeeze through the gap and slip back into the tower.

I run.

I hear Mum's voice calling me. *Ade, Ade, Ade.*

I sprint up the stairs and I pull off the mask and drop the rucksack as I go so I can get to her faster.

When we meet on the stairs, we are both running so fast towards each other that we almost make each other fall over. But we don't fall, we hold each other so close for just a second before we both start running again.

Mum grabs my hand and she doesn't let go. She's stronger than me and she pulls me along with her. For just a split moment I think that there was a time when I was worried I would be the one pulling her from the tower, and that's when I really start running.

Run, run, run. We sprint up the stairs, two at a time.

I don't have time to ask where Dory, Obi and

Ben are. If they have got Pigeon from Dory's flat. If we are all going to be OK. Mum is pulling me so hard up the stairs, up towards the noise of the helicopter.

When we reach the roof, the door is already open. The sound of the helicopter is so loud, it fills my head with its deafening vibrations. The rain lashes down on us and it's hard to keep my eyes open properly.

Suddenly Mum stops pulling me and lets go of my hand. She stands right in front of the doorway, frozen, as though someone has pressed her pause button and she's unable to move forward.

'Mum!' I shout to her, but I don't think she can hear me over the drone of the helicopter. 'Mum!'

Her face looks slack and wax-like, her eyes dull and deadened.

'Please, Mum,' I say. 'Please.'

I hold onto one of her hands and I squeeze it tight. At first it feels lifeless in my fingers, but then I feel Mum squeezing me back. I look up to her and see her face all twisted up as she stares at the helicopter. We take the steps over the doorway, together, side by side, and then we're out on the rooftop, the wind whipping past our faces, making us squint in its force.

I can see the helicopter hovering right next to the roof. There is just a tiny bit of space you have to step over to get from the roof to the helicopter. Inside it, I can see Obi, Dory and Ben's smiling faces, their hands reaching out to me.

I go first. There is a dizzying moment when I look down the gap between the helicopter and the tower. It goes down, down, down. The earth is so far away. I glimpse a flash of the silver-blue of the Bluchers that have reached the tower walls, and then I am in. Dory's arms enclose me. I look around the helicopter cabin, searching for Pigeon among the bodies.

'Where's Pigeon?' I shout, but no one can hear me over the noise of the helicopter's blades. 'Where's Pigeon?' I shout, again. 'Where's Pigeon?'

Only Obi can see I am trying to say something and he leans forward, right towards me, so I can shout directly into his ear. He looks troubled when he hears me but he doesn't look at me. He just stands up from his seat, and as Mum is stepping into the helicopter, Obi jumps out of it. There is a lot of shouting then but no one can hear much of what is being said. No one but me knows what Obi is doing. He runs through the open door and he doesn't look back.

I try to go after him. It was me who should have gone. But Dory and Mum keep holding me between them and I can only cry out for Obi to come back.

My cries are quite lost though. Eaten up by the roaring of the helicopter.

Chapter Fifty-nine

You know how I said that I'd never known time to slow down and stop as much as the moment the Blucher exploded over me? Well, I take that back now. Waiting for Obi to come back is the longest wait of my life. I don't know if he takes five minutes or an hour, but to me, it feels like it will never end.

I remember learning at school how there are 365 days in the year and twenty-four hours in a day and sixty minutes in an hour and sixty seconds in a minute. It feels like every real second that passes is an hour, that every minute is a day.

I can't take my eyes off the open doorway. I can't stop willing Obi to appear through it. But however hard I think it, he doesn't come. No one speaks now. It's just the beating of the helicopter blades and the beating of our hearts.

Then something happens which makes me feel sick from the bottom of my stomach to the top of my head to the toes on my feet. The the roof is moving. A low, ghastly groan comes from the tower itself. It is going to fall.

Just as the top of the roof begins to slant, I see Obi appear in the doorway. A little grey bundle is clasped to his chest. Pigeon.

The helicopter's pilot tries to keep us in line with the falling roof but the gap between us and the tower is much larger now. Obi runs towards us. He runs so fast. He sort of throws Pigeon towards us, and he lightly jumps across the roof into the helicopter.

And then Obi jumps too.

As he leaps from the tower, the building gives way beneath him. It is completely collapsing now.

The helicopter swerves away as the tower crashes downwards and Obi is left flying through the air. Flying in the space between the falling tower and us.

I see his face as he jumps. He isn't scared or panicked like you would imagine him to be. He looks so peaceful, somehow. And happy, perhaps. Happy. I know it doesn't make a lot of sense but that's what I think.

He would have fallen downwards for sure. He would have plummeted down just like those bodies of the pigeons did when Dory and I threw them off the balcony. Or perhaps Obi would have floated softly down, like the feathers.

Gently and softly, making little circles as he went.

But he doesn't fall.

The helicopter moves downwards in such a way that Obi falls onto one of the long poles that are right at the bottom of the helicopter. The bits that look like they are the helicopter's feet. He falls right onto one of them and manages to just hold onto it.

Ben and Mum reach out to him and pull him up into the cabin, right onto our laps.

And as the helicopter rises up into the sky, with the tower crashing down behind us, we all clasp Obi to us.

We hold each other tight.

PART THREE

After

Chapter Sixty

There's a spot at the top of the road where you can just make out the blue line of the sea over the roofs of the buildings. You can't see it if it's foggy or raining hard, but most days, Gaia and I stop to look at it for a moment or two.

It's there today. I mean, I know it's always there, but we can see it today. It sparkles in the sunshine.

Gaia and I walk side by side the rest of the way back home. Gaia talks about what happened at school today but I don't talk much. I like just listening to her voice sometimes.

We go the quick way home, which is past a few shops and down a couple of busy streets. There are so many people on the pavement that at times we have to walk in single file, but we always go back to walking side by side again when there's space. And Gaia doesn't stop talking.

When we first moved here, we could never walk this way because people recognized me and would try to stop us and want to talk to us. Sometimes they were nice people who wanted just to shake my hand, but sometimes I didn't like the way they spoke to me, and that's when Gaia found a long route to school where you didn't run into so many people.

We sort of became a bit famous after we had been rescued, you see. Lots of people wanted to interview us but Obi said he'd rather have stayed in the tower than be on television or in the newspapers, and then none of us wanted to do it after that.

In the end, Obi was quite right about someone else working out how the salt stopped the Bluchers from growing. They discovered that not long after everyone had left the city, and so, after everything, for all the worry about contamination, the Bluchers never made it out of London.

We were the only city to be destroyed.

No one else who stayed, like we did, survived.

Pigeon's doing OK. Although we have a little dog now, called Ollie, who he's not too keen on. Mum takes Ollie for a walk every morning and night, so that's good.

We don't talk about the time Mum didn't go out much, but I just have a feeling it's not going to happen any more.

We see Ben quite often. He likes to walk with Mum and Ollie most evenings. I told him that maybe he should just get a dog too, but he said he likes Ollie well enough, so he'll just walk with them for now.

I see Gaia the most, though.

After we left London, there was only one place I wanted to go. Where Gaia was. And we all ended up staying there.

We eat together a lot, Obi, Dory, Ben, Mum and I. Just like in the old days when we were trapped in the tower. We still eat a lot of pigeon, but now we can have it roasted or in pies and it's just as good as Dory said it was.

We're having dinner tonight, all of us, and Gaia's coming along too. She comes round for a meal most weeks, and sometimes when we are all together, sitting round Dory's table, with Gaia too, I almost forget that she wasn't with us all those times from before. She likes everyone and they like her. She even caught her first pigeon the other week. She didn't want to eat it though.

She let it go before Dory could get the bag out. She told Dory it was an accident, but I saw her lift it up to the sky and let it fly away.

We aren't in the same class any more but it doesn't matter. We just make sure we walk home together and see each other at weekends. We're just down the road from each other again, but not in towers any more. We're just walking towards Gaia's house now.

It has marigolds in pots on the windowsill, and because of their cheerful yellowness, I think it looks like the happiest house on the street. We say goodbye at her gate and I watch Gaia walk towards her door. She always turns round to give me one last smile, and then I watch the door close behind her. I only go when I know she's safely inside.

My house is just a little way down the road. I counted the steps once and got to sixty-eight, which I thought was quite a big number, because to me, it seems like our houses are right next to each other.

Pigeon's waiting for me on the wall and he screeches when he sees me and jumps up onto my shoulder, just like in the old days, in the tower.

The tower feels far away from where we are now. Sometimes I get the feeling that I miss it, but then I think I don't ever want to go back and I'm not sure what the word for that feeling is.

I've come to like living by the sea. I like how its saltiness reminds me of what protected us for all of those days. And I like seeing its blueness all around us.

Only sometimes do I get the jolt of a memory, of being surrounded by a silvery-blue that almost engulfed us.

I have to remind myself that it's just a memory. That it's just the sea I'm seeing.